# TH
# WRONG
# CHILD

Barry Gornell was born in Liverpool and now lives on the West Coast of Scotland. He is a novelist/screenwriter, ex fire-fighter, truck driver and bookshop manager. His short films *Sonny's Pride* and *The Race* were broadcast on STV. Graduating from the University of Glasgow Creative Writing Masters programme in 2008, he was awarded a Scottish Book Trust New Writers Bursary in 2009. His short fiction has been published in *The Herald* and *The Scotsman* newspapers, *Let's Pretend*, *37 stories about (in)fidelity*, *Gutter 03* and *Gutter 04*. *The Healing of Luther Grove* was his first novel, followed by *The Wrong Child*, which was originally published by Scottish press Freight Books in 2016.

# THE
# WRONG
# CHILD

## BARRY GORNELL

ORION

An Orion paperback

First published in Great Britain in 2016 by Freight Books,
This paperback edition published in 2018 by Orion Books
an imprint of The Orion Publishing Group Ltd
Carmelite House, 50 Victoria Embankment,
London EC4Y 0DZ

An Hachette UK Company

1 3 5 7 9 10 8 6 4 2

Copyright © Barry Gornell 2016

Lyrics from 'The Blues You Sang' by James Yorkston. Taken from the LP
*The Cellardyke Recording and Wassailing Society*, 2014, Domino Records.

A CIP catalogue record for this book is
available from the British Library.

ISBN 978 1 4091 7182 9

Typeset by Deltatype Ltd Birkenhead, Merseyside, CH41 4JQ

Printed in Great Britain by CPI Group (UK) Ltd,
Croydon, CR0 4YY

www.orionbooks.co.uk

*Dedicated to*
*Pongo, Eggo, Shy Bollocks and Snooty*

It was the last child's final morning. It broke crisp and clear. The winter sun struggled up the east gable of his isolated clapboard house, illuminating its disrepair. The front of the building was forever sunless. Iron gutters, heavy with weeds and roof tiles, overflowed with icicles. The slow drip of morning thaw fed the stains and rot. The last coat of paint had crackled into a dull glaze and offered scant protection. A mop was frozen into a bucket of murky ice, crusted with fallen leaves beneath a dusting of snow.

In a first-floor window a knife-shaped shard of missing glass revealed a slice of face.

Dog Evans stood at the window, watching through the broken pane. He sweated in the cold. In the mean light that pierced the interior his moist skin appeared translucent, barely containing the blood crawling beneath the surface. His grey eyes and salmon lips were lurid in comparison. Outside, thick rimy frost covered the basin of marsh, part of which separated his home from the rest of the village, away to his right. A common postal code was his only token of inclusion; the occasional delivery his only form of contact.

On the opposite side of the marsh, the harsh November sunshine reflected off the concrete remains of the abandoned schoolhouse. Within those walls, planted in remembrance of the generation lost there, trees thrived. Twenty-two children had been in the class. Twenty-one trees grew in the school.

Dog Evans wanted to be a tree.

# I

He had watched those trees grow, left behind to witness their skyward progress. Out of sight, their young branches had sought each other until they touched, then intertwined, creating a tight ring. The growth of the saplings had been visible through glassless frames; straining ever higher until tousled green tops peered above the walls. One autumn morning, their growth had pushed over a section of the weakened wall, causing the earth to shake in an echo of the explosion that destroyed the building.

The villagers' response to this attempted breakout was to erect a chain-link boundary fence around the memorial. A large white sign with block red letters was planted between wall and wire. The single word 'DANGER' once filled the board, the word itself enough to weigh down the sign and render its footings redundant. The nature of the danger was unspecified. The villagers had stood together, some weeping, some still clinging to teddy bears. They considered the new sign for a while, then walked away, their backs turned.

As time passed, the lower boughs of the nearest trees had grown over the sign, lolling in heavy, insolent swags, twisting it in the first stages of destruction. Dog Evans had watched leafy fingers extend to obscure the first letter. In recent months, ANGER had been its only message and Dog Evans its only reader.

Dog Evans turned the brown Bakelite knob on the bedside radio. He took pleasure in the dull spring-loaded click that preceded the gentle humming of the valves as they grew bright with warmth. They brought the voices into another day. The voices were his company, welcome and invited. He heard the long-gone sing-song of playground and parent, the fractured metre of handclap rhythms and footstep melodies that he was never part of, the skipping rope too fast, the circle exclusive, the ball not his; and laughter. The joyous shouts and shrieks of playtime release shot through his mind like swooping birds, a comfort that caused him to smile and turn to the blur in the mirror.

Dog Evans no longer had a reflection. Moribund blossoms tarnished the silvered glass, their petals spreading as if resisting his image. He had a face that invited blame. Even as a baby, nursed at arm's length, his strange doll-like features had driven away all but the most determined. His appearance had been the start of his mother's isolation, described to others by the midwife, whose visits struck Rebecca Evans as brief and perfunctory. She rarely took her coat off or handled the baby for long, choosing to focus her attention on the mother in order not to have to look upon the child.

Rebecca's determination to breastfeed was encouraged, but was compromised from the start by the baby's strenuous sucking and the extreme soreness of her nipples. It went beyond the pain and tenderness she had been prepared for after the initial seconds of each latching. It lasted the duration, biting and sharp and insistent. The midwife assured her she was doing everything right,

4

that the boy was fully latched on, there was no sign of engorgement and none of the usual causes of discomfort were evident. She advised Rebecca to line the cups of her bra with a cabbage leaf in addition to using the recommended ointments and salves. The leaves helped, soothing between each feed, but did nothing to lessen the dread of the moment she had to take her breast out to stop him wailing. All the good was undone the moment he clamped on, pulling and arching as he drained her.

Within a week her nipples were cracked and bleeding and the ordeal of nursing became intolerable. Rebecca resorted to formula milk. The baby vomited the first bottle and refused to take another, turning away from the rubber teat when it was offered yet howling from hunger.

Weight loss took him back to mother's milk.

Shep came home one evening to find Rebecca crying as the baby guzzled.

'Hey, Becca, come on now.' He held her, looking down at his son. 'I bought new ointment, more cabbage.'

'It's not that,' she said, between sobs.

'Okay, that's good.' Shep dried her cheeks. 'What is it?'

'He's doing it on purpose, hurting me.'

'Hey now, you're tired. It hurts, I know, but—'

'He is, believe me.'

'Rebecca.'

'I'm telling you, Shep.'

'He's a baby. He can't think that way. Look, he's happy, he's even smiling.'

Rebecca frowned as she examined their baby, his face wet with her tears.

'Is that a smile?'

'I think so.'

It was this smile that had caused the teacher, Mr Corrigan, to turn away, convinced it was a sneer, refusing to be riled. The other children noticed, saw it as a chink in the adult world. Dog Evans had enjoyed this power. He saw his peculiarity as a gift. He was never one of them, but he knew he calmed them, his presence akin to snowfall for the children of the one-roomed school. He'd worked by the window, knowing the daily hush that attended his arrival was what truly disturbed the teacher, took away his authority. The pupils ignored Mr Corrigan. They worked hard and excelled as a collective prodigy. Dog Evans would find chocolate or cake on the windowsill where he sat, a sweet within his desk: tokens of gratitude. His innate strangeness precluded any open friendship with other children. There was never a note, nothing traceable, but some anonymous offering. They knew their debt.

On the occasion of Dog's exclusion, the school's first suspension – for reasons kept from the other pupils – he had worked hard in bed, desperate to be back at school. On his return, things had changed. The children had changed. The teacher had reasserted lost authority. Jonny Raffique looked stronger and more defiant. The others gathered around and behind him. Alice Corggie held his hand. They judged Dog that morning, facing him as one alongside the teacher. Speechless, he screamed his loudest at them, at what they had become. He scared them. He was happy when Mr Corrigan confined him to the storeroom. On that first day back, Dog Evans withdrew yet remained: wedged into the rough brick corner of the room. He took comfort from the smells of the virgin materials: graphite, paper, rubber, adhesive and crayons. Pencils of light passed into the space through the ventilation grill fixed head-high in the door. On the other side of the door, the class was working. He was content to watch.

Dog Evans sat at the kitchen table in the dying afternoon, the carcass of his meal barely covering the plate. His hand swept across the tabletop, pinched a stray shard of bone from the Formica surface and forced it between his canine and molar. Pulling it down released a sinewy shred of meat that was sucked free and swallowed. The tip of his tongue rolled around his teeth, checking the space was clear. Another cat leapt up to sit next to him. He stroked the feline, his slender fingers rippling the glossy black fur up to its shoulder blades. The creature lay still on the bench, purring, until a twitch from the whiskers and a flicker in one ear signalled it was time to leave. It stretched as it would after a deep sleep. He took satisfaction from its liquid fall to the floor, its rough tongue as it licked his wrist before disappearing into the kitchen. Dog Evans scratched the pigskin that had been grafted on to his lower arm. The porcine smell, scraped into the dirt beneath his chipped nails, was held up to his nose as a fragrant delicacy.

Leaning back on two legs of the chair, he opened the under-table drawer, took out the only newspaper in the house and spread it flat. The corners of the ancient broadsheet shone with the greasy deposit of years of handling. Blunt marker lines ran through columns of text and advertisements, crossed out as irrelevant, forcing the eye to the single dominant story that ran on almost every page. The accumulated effect of the images of the school's collapse and destruction – distressed parents digging through rubble by hand as snow fell; neighbours holding each other for support and comfort; the wailing faces of the mothers being held back from the covered stretchers by fathers with the weight of death already in their eyes – was compounded by the centre pages. They were a roll call of the dead. Four monochrome rows of fresh faces, young and clean, pristine uniforms washed and ironed, top buttons fastened, ties straight, all ready for the photographer's visit. Each grin, squint, frown, pair of glasses, ponytail, side parting and severe fringe was alive, a sliver of individual character that combined to make up the group's potential. A name and address was printed beneath each child's face, connected to the diagram of the village with a straight line, forming a cat's cradle of grief in which every street, lane, close and wynd was affected. Dog Evans' fingers called at each empty home in turn.

Calvin Struan, 8

*Seven years earlier*

Struan House was the largest residential building on the map and the first any visitor saw upon entering the village. It was set back from the main road at the end of a long gravel path that snaked through acres of topiary and cultivated woodland. Calvin Struan opened the front door and gaped at the heavy flakes of falling snow. A fat child forced into expensive clothes to the detriment of his appearance, Calvin was loud of voice and small of mind, like his father, the laird: landowner and beneficiary of dubious rites of inheritance. Unlike his father, Calvin attended the village school. This break with tradition was in order to assuage the separation anxiety suffered by his clingy mother, who refused to countenance the idea of her boy being dispatched to boarding school, regardless of reputation or expense. Her mollycoddling was merciless. Calvin strove to be a copy of his father, who appeared to him to be in need of no one and nothing. Already tweed-clad and brown-brogued, the boy had assumed the portly bluster of minor gentry with little shame.

On the morning of the tragedy, Calvin was first out of the house, waiting in the front seat of the estate Range Rover to be driven to school. He patted his pockets for the umpteenth time. One held chocolate, the other his lunch money and a similar amount he had taken from his mother's purse for Dog Evans, just in case. He had turned the engine on and the cab was warm by the time his father appeared, his gloved hand clutching a sheaf of brown envelopes. Calvin had read the addresses and knew them to be letters advising of rent rises. He was keen to get to school. He wanted to inform his classmates of the imminent increases before their parents received official notification. He relished the power to affect their day. It would be all pleasure and no responsibility. Like his father, he was impervious to approaches with regard to repair or injustice, as if the 'No Entry' signs about the run-down grandeur of Struan House applied to their persons also.

Passing the gatehouse at the pillared entrance to the property, Calvin noticed the lights were on and smoke rose from both chimneys. The front path was clear of snow. He knew that Jonny Raffique would have done this willingly for his mother without being asked. But that was Jonny, and his mother. Calvin would have liked to do things for Jonny's mother.

Turning on to the main road, Calvin's father stopped the Range Rover at the corner postbox. He pushed the manila envelopes into Calvin's hand and pointed at the box.

'There's a good chap.'

Calvin stepped out of the heated car onto the dirty mound of road-cleared snow. The extra height it afforded him meant he didn't need to stretch to reach the slot. He pushed the letters in as a bundle.

Climbing back into the car, he heard the squeals of

laughter coming from the next house along. He closed the door against them. The Voars were throwing snowballs and their father was joining in the fun, a mini blizzard of swishing arms and white powder as he chased them in circuits around their small rented garden. At the sound of Mr Struan revving away from the kerbside, Maggie Voar looked up and with a squawk of mock panic gathered her two siblings and her father to stand alongside her, forming a human shield. Clearly visible under the street light, yesterday's short, fat snowman had been joined by another, half the height but just as stout. The Voars tried not to giggle as they lined up in front of them, elbowing each other as the Struans passed by. Robbie and Cameron surprised Maggie by daring to wave. Calvin could see the two snowmen they were trying to conceal. He had no doubt whom they represented. His father snorted, dismissing their childish insult.

'Postman will soon wipe the smiles from their faces, don't you think?'

Calvin turned to sneer at Maggie as he pictured the brown envelope arriving with the white of early Christmas cards. He felt better when he saw the joy slip from her face.

Calvin's father winked at his son.

Red-eyed with grief and lairdly anger, Ruaridh Struan had been the first parent to voice it: 'Why did it have to be him?'

# 2

Shep Evans withdrew the notes from the cash machine. Folding them into his palm to stop the wind stealing them away, he crossed the main street of the seaside town to the post office.

Inside, his pen hovered over the pad of writing paper. Looking above the service counter, he saw the date on the electronic calendar.

'This is a bank holiday weekend, isn't it?'

'You bet,' answered the guy at the counter, obviously pleased. 'I've got three days of fishing ahead of me.'

'This time of year?'

'Cod's coming through.'

'You must enjoy your fishing.'

'Enjoy the catching even more. And you can only catch them when they're here.'

'Need to use the window you're given.'

'Absolutely.'

'Likewise,' said Shep, indicating the pad he was about to write on. 'When will this arrive, if I post it now?'

'You'll catch the last collection, but it'll still be Tuesday at the earliest.'

'Okay. Fingers crossed for that then.'

Shep returned to the pad. He clicked the ballpoint down and wrote, 'I hope this gets to you for your birthday', having been told that it wouldn't. He signed with the swirl of an S. Teasing the paper from the pad, he wrapped it around the banknotes and slid it into an envelope he had already addressed.

When he pushed it across the counter, the postmaster, according to his lapel badge, saw the address and raised his eyebrows.

'Tuesday's optimistic.'

'I know. I forgot about the holiday.'

'Special occasion?'

'It is, yes.'

'You want it recorded, proof of posting? I happened to see it was cash.' The postmaster held the envelope in his hand and gave Shep a look that said he thought this would be the best option, for peace of mind.

'No, seeing you take it is all the proof I need, thank you.'

'If you're sure.'

'I am.'

The man weighed and stamped the envelope, then dropped it into a postal sack. He was about to ring the sale when he saw Shep scanning the gift counter.

'Get you anything else?'

'Your best box of chocolates.' Shep pulled a large note from his wallet.

Leaving the chocolates with his briefcase in the passenger footwell, Shep took a cigar from a tin in the glove compartment, locked the car and cut between the shops, through to the promenade.

He sat in a shelter and smoked as he watched redshank and ringed plover at the water's edge, mincing up and down the tideline, feeding on whatever the waves had left behind. A yappy mongrel puppy triggered the *kyip, kyip, kyip* of the redshank's alarm call and the instant departure of all the birds, a low cloud, wing-points skimming the water on their way to a safer stretch of shore. The pup splashed after them, closely followed by a shrieking toddler in wellington boots and flapping jacket, impervious to the bitter conditions, waving a plastic spade at the now distant flock. His parents hugged each other as they walked, enjoying their son's glee. Shep took a final draw, rolled the smoke around his mouth, let it go, tapped the cigar out on the concrete wall and left the shelter.

Rebecca was waiting for Shep. She blew him a kiss and waved from the front window as he pulled onto the driveway. He couldn't help but cheer up.

'Hi,' she said, opening the door for him.

'Hi to you too.'

She kissed him, put her arms around him and hugged him on the doorstep.

'Happy to see me?'

'Every time.'

Shep took a step back and admired his wife.

'You're a sight for sore ones.'

'I made a special effort for you.'

'There's no need, but I'm glad you did.'

'My pleasure.'

Shep handed her the chocolates.

'For me?'

'Who else?'

She grinned at him. 'What about my figure?'

'It would take more than a box of chocolates to knock you out of shape.'

She giggled as she dragged him inside. 'Come on in, we're letting all the heat out.'

Shep hung his coat up in the porch, slipped his boots off and followed her down the hallway into the kitchen in his stockinged feet.

'Becca?'

'Yes,' she said, looking up from the whisky she was pouring for him.

'You want to do something this weekend?'

'Such as?'

'Go for a meal, watch a film, a play maybe. All of those if you like.'

She put the bottle down. There was a trace of sadness in her smile as she walked over to Shep and kissed him.

'You're so sweet, you know that?'

'How so?'

'Working all week and still making time to be thinking about me.'

'I never stop thinking about you.'

He took her face in his hand, his thumb brushing the scar at the corner of her eye.

'Maybe not this weekend,' she said.

'You sure?'

'Yes.'

Shep gathered Rebecca into him. He held her close enough to feel the tremors, but he couldn't stop them.

Dog Evans traced the road of the newspaper's centre-page map to where it stopped at the school on the right-hand edge of the marsh. There was no indication that the road also forked to the left; no mention of him, the sole survivor, or his parents and the house they had shared.

This exclusion had begun that distant yet immediate day, as the fallout still clogged the air, drying mouths and stinging eyes in the incessant snowfall, filling noses and impregnating the clothes and minds of every witness.

Dog Evans recalled hearing the growing murmur that had risen to muted cries of joy and a rush of bodies when it was discovered someone had survived. Their child, please God, theirs. But hope imploded as he, the wrong child, was dragged from the bunker of the storeroom that had protected him, in tattered clothing, his hair singed and a flap of skin the length of his lower arm hanging from wrist to knee. As soon as they had him clear of the wreckage, they let go, their moral obligation to life paid. Needy faces stared at his survival, unable to embrace it. It mocked their loss, the loss of good children. They stepped back as he slowly came to, blinking, focusing, balancing, noticing the wound to his arm. Dog Evans examined the dangling flap of skin; poked his exposed flesh, fascinated. Wind gusted grit, dust and snow across those stricken faces still watching him. Others were crouched over or holding the dead, sobbing and moaning, or pulling at rubble in the hope of finding another alive, one worthy of life.

His cough hacked and rattled through his grime-filled chest, until it cleared into a wheezy laugh of surprise and validation. There was something victorious in the way he smiled at his audience.

'It's my birthday,' he said.

The villagers darkened as a wordless blame congealed around the one who lived.

A fox crossed the space between them, a grey-brown bird in its mouth, a wing trailing, its head bouncing. Dog pointed at it and looked around for his dad to identify the bird. He wasn't there. Neither was his mum.

Dog Evans hadn't seen his parents for a long time. They were never there when he came down in the morning, always there when he lay upstairs at night, their voices murmuring, their words just out of earshot. He'd sit up in bed to listen, cocking his head, leaning over to put his ear to the floor, desperate to hear, to understand. Occasionally, he would pull back his blankets to go to them. But each time, as he put his weight on his feet to stand, their conversation stopped, as if for adult ears only. He'd creep to the top of the stairs to stand in threadbare pyjamas, waiting for them to call him. He would sometimes stand for hours before returning to bed. Those rare nights that the need to see them was overwhelming, he would fix a welcome on his face and continue down, wide-eyed with hope. The room would always be empty; the coals on the fire dull beneath a layer of fallen soot. His smile would tighten, his teeth retreat behind bulbous lips as he felt the twist of ache in his chest. The hardened soles of his feet sanded the wooden treads as he climbed back to his room. Beneath the sheets, he would hear again their distant voices, once more out of their hiding place.

Tonight, Dog Evans lit a fire for the parents he had waited long enough for. It caught quickly. The flames raced deep into the bone-dry tinder. Freshly crumpled images of children became spectral within the smoke as the draw of the chimney pulled them skyward.

Dog Evans rested the rusty spade on the satchel strap

in the bowl of his shoulder. Leaving his home, he picked his way from tussock to tussock across the marsh to the school, taking as direct a line as possible. His footsteps left dark imprints as they crushed the ice crystals that had formed a crisp cover over the sphagnum moss.

He passed through the broken fence, unseen.

Looking back for the last time, he smiled when he saw the glow of the fire in the window. Ascending ghosts unwound from the chimney stack. The marsh sparkled beneath the waxing gibbous moon.

To his left, the houses at the rear of the village looked permanently closed. The buildings presented a solid defence of lifeless walls. Doorways were bricked up and shutters screwed tight across windows painted blind. These sightless facades bore no relation to their whitewashed other halves. Dog Evans, on nights when he had limped furtive through the village, had seen the other, desperately optimistic side of these houses. He had gazed through the landscape windows that opened up their fronts, broad in compensation for their shuttered backs. He had observed watchful parents spoiling replacement children behind glazing that reflected the sun's arc, allowed light in and desires out. To Dog Evans, the village appeared anchored to the site of the schoolhouse while at the same time pulling away, like a tethered hound straining against its leash.

The soft fronds of the lower boughs brushed him as he moved into the trees. The mass of determined foliage had blocked out the sun, created a crackling carpet of dry leaves, needles and twigs, where scaled creatures slithered and fed. He sensed welcome ahead. He stopped. As he stood with the trees, he could hear the scratch of pencil on jotter paper, smell the polished wood of the classroom floor and feel the reflected sunlight. He entered the small glade, now less than half the size of the single classroom. Smiling children looked up at him before returning to their work, heads down in concentration. In a handful of steps, Dog Evans stood in the middle, among friends.

The spade split the green skin of the earth. Two straight lines the length of a child's body bisected each other. Forcing the spade beneath the grass, shallow and flat, he sliced through tender roots, separating the turf from the topsoil. Folding four triangular flaps away from each other, he exposed a dark square of sweet loam and plunged the blade into the centre. He stopped when the hole was deep enough.

Satchel, shirt and trousers all slipped easily from his frame.

Dog Evans stood naked at the end of his last day. The four flaps now pointed to his planted form, a spent jack-in-the-box. His discarded clothing cushioned the soles of his buried feet, his knees invisible within the hand-packed soil. He looked to the stars in the clear night sky. Moonlight flooded the glade, making filigree of the frosted grass and highlighting the stomach scars that ripped across his bright, hairless body. He lifted his hand to his mouth. His Adam's apple pulsed as he swallowed a plump worm. Save for the rustle of minor life in the inky lunar shadows, all he could hear was the growing of the trees, the sluggish flow of seasonal sap along meshing branches. As the worm writhed in his gullet, a contrary peristalsis, Dog Evans began to take root, to rejoin the class.

MaggieVoar, 11    Robbie Voar, 6    Cameron Voar, 6

*Seven years earlier*

Maggie had caught the look on Calvin's face. It made her feel sad. Other people's misfortune made him happy.

She hid her misgivings as she looked back to the house at the playful chastising of her mum's voice.

'You're a bigger kid than they are, you know that,' said Mairi. 'You shouldn't be encouraging them.'

She was leaning against the door frame, a cup of tea steaming in her hand. Maggie feigned happiness as her dad played the innocent.

'Hey, nothing to do with me. It was built before I came out.'

'Really? And who was it set the bad example by building the big one yesterday?'

'She's got you there, Dad,' said Maggie.

'Traitor,' said John Voar, scooping a broad palm of snow into Maggie's face. 'I thought we were on the same side.'

Robbie and Cameron fell about laughing as Maggie squawked and spat and wiped her face. She gathered herself and gave her dad as stern a look as she could muster.

'We don't take sides in this family.'

'You tell him, Maggie,' said her mum, 'and John,

can you lift those two eejits, they're like wee snowmen themselves.'

John Voar lifted a twin in each arm and shook them in the air, white clumps falling from their parkas as the three of them bounced up and down, filling the morning with the noise of play.

'John, can you behave, you'll have them vomiting their breakfasts, honestly.'

John paid no heed, cheerfully defiant as he continued to shake each boisterous bundle, squirming and flailing, slipping from their winter clothing.

'John.'

'Right,' he said, putting them down, 'kiss for Mum, then school, do some learning.'

The two released boys pulled their trousers up as they ran to their mum. Maggie hugged her dad. When they had been tucked in again, Robbie and Cameron ran down the path and John joined Mairi in the doorway, his arm around her.

'Got everything you need?' she said as the twins pushed through the gate.

'Yes,' chimed Robbie and Cameron.

'You sure?'

They turned to see their mum holding up two lunch-boxes.

Maggie shook her head in cahoots with her parents as the two boys trudged back.

'Thank you,' they said as they took their boxes.

'You're welcome. Hurry up now, you don't want to be late.'

'And Maggie's in charge,' said John.

'We know,' they said as they ran back to their waiting sister, waving to their mum and dad for the last time.

Outside the classroom, Maggie Voar's voice carried the authority of her parents. She was adept at moderating Robbie and Cameron's sibling outbursts, curbing the noise levels and anarchist tendencies of their youth with mention of other people and the respect they were due. Robbie and Cameron idolised her. Only two years older than them, she was nonetheless their natural guide through life in the absence of their parents. So much so that at times the boys gave the impression of having a glide in the eye, such was their continual sideways checking for Maggie's approval or opprobrium.

Breathless and red-cheeked from the exertions of the snow fight, the twins were nevertheless subdued by Maggie's silence as they left the garden to head for school that morning. Usually joined at the hip, the two of them separated and each took one of their sister's hands as they walked into the village.

'Maggie?'

'Yes.'

'Are you okay?'

'Of course. Why do you ask?'

'You're not talking.'

Maggie gave both the boys' hands a wee press, keeping her counsel about Calvin Struan. They wouldn't understand.

'I'm listening,' she said. 'I like the way the snow steals away all the sound.'

The boys looked around, suddenly aware of how quiet the village was. They both stole a glance up at Maggie, then at each other, and smiled. The three of them continued on without a word.

They paused for a second at the Todds' house. Two sets of footprints led through the gate and on ahead. The Todds were just visible beneath the street lights, like smudges in their black duffle coats, labouring through the heavy snow. Maggie thought one of them looked back as they reached the top of Main Street, but couldn't be sure. She waved, just in case. Robbie and Cameron followed suit with their free hands, but the Todds turned the corner and were out of sight. The twins pulled at Maggie and they all picked up a little speed, so keen were the boys to catch their friends.

Robbie and Cameron fell into following the Todds' footprints exactly, quiet in their absorption for a while. When Robbie spoke, his voice was uncertain.

'Maggie?'

'Yes.'

'Do you think Dog will be in school today?'

'I imagine so, why?'

'He got sent home.'

'Doesn't it last forever?' asked Cameron.

'I don't think so,' she said.

The two boys were thoughtful as they took this in.

'He scares me.'

'And me,' said Cameron.

'I didn't like when he screamed.'

'No,' said Maggie. 'That wasn't nice.'

'Calvin weed his pants,' said Robbie, leaning forward and looking at Cameron to share his pleasure.

'Hey, it's not nice to laugh at other people, you two.'

Both boys pulled their heads back.

'Why isn't Dog at the big school?' asked Robbie.

'He's a teenager,' added Cameron.

'Only just,' said Maggie. 'Dad said he got kept back.'

'Kept back?'

'Because he's not ready for the big school yet.'

'Not ready?'

'Yes, not ready.'

A few seconds passed.

'What does that mean?'

'It just means he's not ready,' said Maggie, her tone closing the conversation. 'Come on, let's catch up with Ronah and Jack.'

She pulled on their hands and started to run, shouting at them to keep in their steps, keep up; keep in their steps, keep up, half dragging them along. Robbie and Cameron snapped out of their fear, laughing and sliding as they high-stepped and quick-stepped to keep up with Maggie and catch the Todds.

The Voars and the Todds arrived at school together. Calvin was waiting for them at the gate. He wasn't hogging the shelter of the school doorway as usual. Maggie cried when he told her about the impending rent increase and she had to restrain Robbie and Cameron from hitting him for causing her tears.

'Why?' she said. 'You don't need any more money, you're already rich.'

'Mummy spends it, so Daddy needs to get more. That's how it works,' he said.

'But you like doing this, why?'

'I'm supposed to.'

Maggie wiped her eyes. 'You're going to spend the rest of your life making people unhappy.'

She glared at Calvin for a moment before leading Robbie and Cameron away.

The Todds remained, staring at Calvin, unblinking, until he looked less pleased with himself. A snowball arrived, thrown fast and true, bursting in a *pluff* of sharp crystals the moment it skelped the side of Calvin's face. By the time Calvin spun around, there were other children gathering handfuls of snow and it wasn't possible to point the finger at any individual. He hardened his face to stop his bottom lip quivering, but he had no control over the fat teardrop that glistened as it fell. Maggie stuck her tongue out at him, as did Robbie and Cameron. Robbie was emboldened.

'Wee pants.'

Maggie didn't tell him off. Cameron copied his brother.

'Wee pants.'

'Wee pants, wee pants, wee pants, wee pants ...'

Others in the playground joined in, pointing at Calvin through the falling snow, and he could do nothing but stand alone. Maggie enjoyed his isolation.

Searching beyond Calvin, across the marsh, she hoped for signs of Mr Corrigan's car. She wanted to be in school.

On days of fine weather, the Voars viewed the classroom as a necessary cage. Voracious for education, they reined in their kinetic vitality in order to study, both their parents having impressed upon them the freedom gained through learning. 'Knowledge is a companion,' their clear-eyed father insisted. His roaming intellect kept him company on the wards and corridors of the community hospital where he was a porter and their mother was a nurse. The Voars' relentless questioning, which the teacher frequently found tiring, wasn't born of belligerence but the need to understand.

Returning home at the end of the school day, they would usually be quizzed by their parents over the dinner table, to establish the worth of the day's teaching. The children would joust and compete to present something and a benign form of home schooling would continue as they ate; their parents adding to what they had learned. And whatever was left of the day they would use, until exhausted or gathered in, to be held and carried to bed.

Today, Maggie saw the school as a refuge, an escape from Calvin Struan and the bad news that lay in store. Her parents would be able to tell there was something wrong and she wouldn't be able to hide it. She would be the one to give them the bad news. As the wind spun the snow, she moved with Ronah to their usual playground place.

# 3

Father Wittin was about to follow them inside when he heard voices and a shuffling of feet around to the left of the church. Leaning out of the stone arch doorway he caught sight of Deborah Cutter, hiding herself in the shadows. He couldn't see anyone else.

'Deborah?'

'Father?'

'Is someone annoying you out there?'

'No, Father.'

'You sure now? I thought I heard talking.'

She didn't answer. He went outside.

'Deborah,' he said. 'Come in now, why don't you?'

'Why? They don't want me to.'

'It's not their church. Now come on in.'

After some hesitation, she stepped into the porch light. She faced him, her hand open by her side as if holding onto a child. He held his own hand out. She came to him and entered the foyer, brushing against him as he held the door for her, leaving just enough room. She didn't smell as though she'd been drinking.

'I'll just sit at the back.'

'Sure, that's grand,' he said, giving her arm a brief squeeze. 'Don't you be letting them make you feel you have no right to be part of this, okay?'

'Okay. Thank you, Father.'

'Okay, now.'

Deborah took a back pew as Wittin strode down the aisle.

It struck him, as he stood before the gathering (they could hardly be called a congregation), that Deborah was the only one who really wanted to be here. Her little white face shone from the back, a moon rising over a field of solemn heads. This night was the only time in the year that his pews were anything close to being fully occupied. Even Christmas had the air of a sorrowful ritual. He was, privately, of the opinion that it was only its isolation, its position as an outpost of faith, that stopped the church from pulling the plug altogether on this diocese, instead of using the posting as a form of punishment. He was certainly out of the way.

Wittin wasn't ashamed that his short sermon was similar to the one that he'd used last year, and the year before. It hadn't changed much since the first, six years ago, the year after the accident, when the priest he replaced had finally lost his mind and abandoned his fold. He'd given up trying to find new words to deal with this day, words they'd listen to anyway. One or two made the sign of the cross when they were sure he'd finished. Most merely shuffled out. None acknowledged Deborah, not even John Cutter. Some of the men went so far as to walk down the side of the aisle furthest from her; an act as shameful as any Wittin had seen in his time here.

Outside, an avenue of candles lined the sloped tarmac apron that led up to the church, one on each grave. The children had been buried in two rows, either side of the broad path. As beautiful as it looked tonight, Wittin was convinced that this was why many of those that did attend chose to use the side door that led out onto the cemetery proper. It wasn't the dead. It was those dead.

They were already lighting their procession candles, the flames protected from what breeze there was by a paper cup shield, which also served to stop the molten wax dripping down their hands. Without a leader to speak of, they simply moved away in a silent huddle, heading down Main Street, through the village and out to the school, where they would huddle together again in a vigil that to his mind did more harm than good. Wittin let them get a good head-start. He lit a cigarette and closed his eyes during the long, slow exhalation through his nose.

'Why do you come? You don't want to.'

He'd forgotten about Deborah.

'I'm their priest,' he said. 'I should be there. It's my job.' He offered her the packet. She took one and lit it from his. 'They might need me, even if they don't want me.'

'That's something, I suppose.'

She lit her candle and they followed the rest, the shepherd and the lost sheep, not trying too hard to catch up.

Adrift in her own loss, Deborah only realised she had caught up with them when she bumped into Mary Magnal. The collision ripped the base of her paper cup. The hot wax that leaked out and ran across the back of her hand took Deborah's mind off Mary's sour tutting and frantic checking that her Sunday coat hadn't been damaged.

They were at the chain-link fence that protected

them from the school. It was taking longer than usual to get everybody through. Some were already within its perimeter, while others waited outside, straining to see over them and find out what the hold-up was. Their backs were to her and there was a mumble of disbelief passing backwards from the front that convinced her they were about to turn around and tell her she wasn't welcome. She looked back; the priest was still another twenty yards behind her, reluctance in every step. Anxiety puckered her eyes closed and tightened her grip around her candle.

She only opened her eyes when she felt the priest's hand resting on hers. By which time Mary Magnal was stepping through the fence.

When Deborah arrived, she wished she hadn't. They weren't together as usual. There was no collective support. They were strung around the space like a cordon, staring, incredulous, at the same thing.

Ronah Todd, 10 Jack Todd, 8

*Seven years earlier*

Ronah Todd stood alongside her brother Jack. They stared at Calvin Struan as he wiped tears and ice from a reddening face. It was almost a look of pity. They wore spectacles, steel-rimmed and thick-lensed, the deep convexity of which had the effect of presenting their eyes to the world as if held open. Magnified into a state of constant awareness and scrutiny, they hovered above their ever-ready smiles of slightly bucked teeth, hemmed in by dimples. Calvin looked away, uncomfortable under the Todds' stare. Old for their years, as the adults said.

They'd been adopted as babies and raised by the Red Todds, the only communist family in the village. Both had been brought up to sing 'The Red Flag' instead of praying, which, the teacher insisted, they were required to do outside the classroom, sometimes in the rain. Although they refused to draw the Saltire on St Andrew's Day, rejecting both religion and nationalism as crutches for the weak, they were keen readers of Robert Burns because their adoptive parents said he was one of the most widely read poets in Russia.

There was nothing frivolous about the way they acted or dressed. Their boots were always polished, from the toe to the heel, the laces to the welt, though the soles were sometimes over-worn. Skirts and trousers, washed and ironed, could be too short for too long before replacement, depending upon when exactly during the school term the growth spurt took place. Their wardrobe was simple and broadly seasonal.

They respected the workers – which meant their parents, employees of the Struan estate – and had been made aware of the limitations that often came with that work. They were the only conspicuous sharers of sweets, biscuits or fruit with Dog Evans and they came to no harm. They were not bullied because they couldn't help it or be blamed. They were just children.

'She's right, you know,' said Ronah.

'What?' said Calvin.

'If you don't change your ways, you will be responsible for other people's misery.'

'Go away. Father says you're silly.'

'Your father is wrong.'

'But he's the laird.'

'That's silly.'

Jack and Ronah grinned at each other.

'Stop laughing at Father.'

'We're not.'

'We're laughing at what you said.'

'Your father isn't funny.'

Ronah offered Calvin a tissue from her pocket.

'You should blow your nose.'

Calvin ignored the tissue. Ronah shrugged, then she and Jack turned and walked away from him towards the rest of the class.

# 4

Dog Evans had opened his eyes at the sound of approaching footsteps. In the dark interior of the trees, lights flickered as they drew close. A disembodied face fluttered above each flame. He smiled. The children had come, stepping from their own storeroom back into the classroom. All he had ever wanted. But now they hesitated. Candlelit faces shimmered like waiting souls. There were many more than twenty-one. There was a silence of disbelief amongst these people who had stumbled without warning into the past. He could hear weeping. He saw moonlight in tears coursing down lambent cheeks. Pain and turmoil weakened the voice that asked him, 'Why are you here?'

'It's my birthday,' he said, smiling at Jenny Cutter's mum.

Deborah Cutter covered the dark space of her mouth, suffocating her response.

Dog Evans didn't hear the branch on its sweeping trajectory; or the crack of his skull and splinter of his teeth as his head was punched forwards and down, his chin driving into his chest.

Wittin saw candles fall from shock-slackened hands and splutter on the ground as the body lurched forward, extinguished. John Cutter let the makeshift club drop to his side but retained his hold. He heaved with release as the knees of Dog Evans snapped and twisted under the dead weight of his torso. The witnesses, many hiding their faces, were privy to the sound of the elastic rupture of tendon and cartilage, sharper than the snap of a falling tree. John Cutter shed tears like sap, slow and from the core. A pitiful keening escaped from him, childlike and unbearable. He was held, his face drawn into the heavily coated chest of Ruaridh Struan, who murmured something about justice as Cutter's call to the dead was smothered within olive herringbone.

The remaining villagers contracted around the twisted form of the once-surviving child. They didn't stare for long.

'We need to get rid, out of sight.'

Nobody told Ruaridh Struan he was wrong.

John Longfield took the initiative. He knelt beside Dog Evans and gripped a handful of the sod with his farmer's paw, ready to peel it away from the body. A tap on his back caused him to pause. Dr Corggie placed two flat fingertips on the boy's wrist. When he was satisfied there was no pulse, he put the hand back on the ground.

'Okay.'

John Longfield removed the sod. Nugget Storrie followed his lead, pulling another corner away. Dr Corggie and Robert Walker stripped the remaining quarters back as Ruaridh Struan picked up Dog's spade.

'What do you think you're doing?' said Father Wittin.

He was universally ignored.

'Enough now, I'm telling you. You think I won't say anything; that you'll actually get away with this?'

As Wittin rushed to stop them, John Cutter swung

the club again, smacking flat across the priest's stomach, taking his speech from him.

'Do what you need to do,' said Cutter as Wittin stumbled backwards, the nearest tree halting any fall and knocking the last of the wind from his body. He slid down the trunk, mouth gaping, struggling to catch his breath, looking on, horrified, as they proceeded to bury the remains.

Ruaridh Struan began, sweat soaking through his tweeds as he moved the dirt away. Tina Louise Raffique took it from him and contributed with a few spadefuls. From her it was passed from hand to dirty hand in village complicity as the soil around the boy was cleared afresh. They scraped and dug and swore and laughed and the hole grew deeper and wider. Eventually Dog Evans' body crumpled to the bottom on top of his clothing. He was then covered with the dirt; his cooling corpse inhumed without being handled. Many willing feet tamped down the corners of turf.

Wittin felt totally alone. He closed his eyes to the desecration before him; the small circle of trees planted in memory of lost childhood being poisoned from the heart with the death of another innocent. When he opened them, he was searching up through the criss-cross of branches for shifting flecks of the starry sky and beyond.

'Lord, help me. I am sick unto death of dead children, the parents of dead children and this sour little village whose name is synonymous with dead children. Sure, this whole fucking village is misery distilled.' He lowered his gaze to the crime scene. 'Will you look at them?'

The ground they stood on was flat and had a dull

sheen of forced compression. Even though tears were still being shed, there was happiness in the snivelling and nose-wiping, restrained hoots born of disbelief and tinged with desperation, accompanied by hugs, arm slaps and pulled punches in a scrum of togetherness, the steam of their exertion rising through their breath in the moon's light; and kisses, congratulatory, liberating.

'This is the happiest I've ever seen them, stamping on the grave of a child.' He got to his feet. 'Is it any wonder they don't attend? They don't believe. They can't allow that their children are in a better place, an everlasting life.'

When they had finished their bonding, an unspoken acknowledgement of their deed, the villagers turned to leave. Feeling empty of conviction, Wittin moved to stand astride the path. He raised his hands to stop them. He was thankful they paused, some bowing their heads.

'We should at least say a prayer,' he said.

Seeing the confusion on their faces as they looked at him, he was stunned to realise that they had been expecting his benediction. It was his turn to laugh, aghast. 'You want my blessing, after what you've just done? Sure, there isn't a true Christian among you. There can be no forgiveness.' They were already moving away. 'Do you rejoice that your children are in heaven?' he asked. Angry turns of the head, a hardening of stance and the resentment of their stares showed they didn't. 'Well, I do.' He pointed to the fresh grave. 'And that poor child is with them now.'

Mary Magnal moved quickly to slap him across the face. Further violence hung in the air. His cheek stung as he saw himself reflected in Mary's spectacles. Her chin was firm below tight thin lips.

'I'll be taking confessions,' he said to them all. 'Tonight. All night, if needs be.'

Twigs cracked underfoot as they left him behind.

Deborah looked back briefly, yet left with them nonetheless.

At the grave, Wittin picked the spade up and drove it into the ground, the only headstone Dog Evans would be getting. He went to put his hands in his pockets against the cold but stopped himself. He joined them, raised them to his chest and after a moment bowed his head.

'Lord, make us instruments of your peace. Where there is hatred, let us sow love; where there is injury, pardon; where there is discord, union; where there is doubt, faith; where there is despair, hope; where there is darkness, light; where there is sadness, joy. Grant that we may not so much seek to be consoled as to console; to be understood as to understand; to be loved as to love. For it is in giving that we receive; it is in pardoning that we are pardoned; and it is in dying that we are born into eternal life.' He sighed, as if the prayer was inadequate. 'Sorry it was so general. I didn't know you. Sure I'd say it was more for those left behind than yourself. Those needing it.'

Wittin crossed himself, found the warmth of his pockets and left.

Norrie Storrie, 7

*Seven years earlier*

Ed Munson looked up from the newspaper opened out on his counter as the paperboy, Norrie Storrie, came back into the shop at the end of his round. Norrie lifted the empty delivery bag over his head, careful not to dislodge his woolly hat or get tangled with his binoculars, and handed it to Munson.

'Good man, Norrie,' Munson said. 'Not easy when it's heavy going underfoot, is it?'

Norrie shook his head, sending the dewdrop from the end of his cold red nose away to his left, where it landed on the tiled floor. Munson's Scottie dog, Ivor, left the warmth of his basket next to the storage heater to lick at the drop. Norrie stamped his feet and pulled the mitten covers of his fingerless gloves back over the ends of his frozen fingers.

'Still snowing, I see.'

'Aye.'

'Three days now.'

'Aye.'

Ivor returned to his basket.

Norrie blew warm air into his cupped hands.

'Why don't you get a heat?'

Norrie stood next to Ivor and placed his hands on top of the heater.

'Manage to see anything?'

'Not really,' said Norrie, sniffing. 'I saw the barn owl again, over at the graveyard.'

'She'll be struggling to find food, with all the snow.'

'I would say so, aye. Oh, and a heron, down at the edge of the marsh, spearing something he was.' Norrie looked up at Munson. 'What would a heron be spearing in the middle of winter?'

'I couldn't say, Norrie. That's your area of expertise.'

'I'll find out, let you know tomorrow, in case anybody asks.' Norrie bent to give Ivor's head a wee rub.

'You do that,' said Munson. 'Anything else?'

Norrie hesitated for a moment. His face flushed, redder than it had been from the cold. He stepped closer and whispered, 'Alice Corggie. She's outside.'

'Oh, I see,' said Munson, his voice low as he leaned over the counter to Norrie. 'And she's some bird, wouldn't you say?'

Clamping his mouth tight, trying not to laugh, Norrie snorted, sending another watery dribble down into the left eyepiece of his binoculars. The old man chuckled as he reached beneath the counter and handed the flustered boy a pack of tissues.

'Here, take these.'

Norrie took the tissues and pulled at the cellophane wrapper.

'See you tomorrow, okay?'

'Okay, thanks, Mr Munson.'

Norrie was still cackling as he walked away, pulling a tissue from the packet and wiping the snot-wet from the lens. He turned in the doorway and looked back through the cleaned sights to see a magnified Ed Munson put his finger over his lips and gesture to where Alice Corggie was standing, feet away. Norrie covered his own lips, sealing the pact. Munson was smiling as he returned his attention to his newspaper.

# 5

Nobody spoke as they left the burial behind, dispersing through the village, eyes to the ground, soiled hands hidden in winter coats. The further Nugget and Lynne Storrie walked, the more the footfalls of the others faded. Turning onto the driveway to their home, they could hear Bru's whimpering cutting into the quiet of the night and see him waiting in the light that leaked beneath the door.

'Shit,' said Nugget, 'listen to him. He must be wondering what he's done wrong. I don't think he's ever been locked in on his own before, has he?'

'I doubt it,' said Lynne. She gave Nugget a raised-eyebrow look. 'That's not like you at all. Why did you?'

'I didn't want him following us. He's still a puppy really.'

'Wise move, Nug. Especially after what happened. He'd be digging him up again.'

'Ugh, Lynne. Jeez.'

Nugget unlocked the door. He opened it carefully so as not to catch Bru's claws, scratching at the gap. Lynne went past him into the house as Bru jumped up to greet him, licking his unshaven neck and jawline, causing Nugget to laugh and push him away, back to the floor. When he stood up from stroking the dog, Lynne threw his mailbag at him and he was forced to take a step back to catch it. He looked at it, he looked at Bru; he looked at her.

'Lynne?'

'Well, you know what you need to do,' she said. 'What are you waiting for?'

His eyes widened.

'Really? You think I should go now, so soon?'

'Why not? He won't be going home any more, will he?'

'But …' He shifted, discomfited by Lynne's request. 'Don't you feel bad, even a little bit?'

'Nug, I feel poor, a lot.'

'But.'

'No buts,' she said, sliding open the frosted-glass door on the dresser, revealing their drink store. She dropped a half-bottle of whisky into the bag. 'You've been pushing those packages through his door for years now.'

The packages were always the same size and weight. Occasionally the envelopes changed colour, when a packet had been finished maybe, or when the sender couldn't lay his hands on his usual supply. The postmark was rarely the same, coming from all over the country. It was obvious what they contained; so obvious that one time Nugget had opened one to check. He had found a slim bale of banknotes wrapped in a piece of paper, plain save for the line 'Buy a good thing' and the swirl of an S in the bottom right corner.

The moment Nugget knew, his behaviour changed. He was first into the depot, waiting for the van. He kept the packages secret from the other two postmen. They were delighted, coming in every day to a pre-sorted route. Nugget rejoiced when the office was downsized and, due to his impressive work regime, he became the sole full-time postman for the village.

'You know it's there,' said Lynne. 'What if someone else knows about it?'

'Nobody else knows; how could they?'

'We can't be sure.'

When Lynne and Nugget had been away on a rare visit to Lynne's family two years ago, the substitute postman had handled one of the envelopes. Suspecting what it was and being tempted, he'd taken it to the tavern rather than post it. He was pondering the likelihood of getting away with it while he drank when the barman caught him unawares. When asked outright, the postman told him, 'I think it's money.' The barman felt the envelope out of curiosity. On seeing the address, he dropped it instantly. The substitute had no option but to deliver.

Upon his return, Nugget played dumb, as curious as the barman. He managed to shift attention by being annoyed at the substitute bringing somebody's private mail into the tavern. The barman agreed and conversation moved on. But Lynne was right. It was at the back of some minds. Sooner or later, others would come for it.

'Just in case,' he said. 'I should get there first.'

Lynne was pleased.

'Go and get it,' she said, patting the bag.

He was still watching her hand when it stopped and he knew she was staring at him.

'Doesn't it feel disrespectful to you?' he said. 'So soon?'

'Was there any respect in the killing and the burying?'

Bru's claws clicked on the linoleum floor.

'You think it's wise, though? Really?'

'Oh please, tonight of all nights, show me some of the old Nugget.' She softened her voice as her hand crept up his leg and cupped his crotch. 'Some of the old spunk.' Her filthy smile spread wide in response to his grin. 'You still got it in you?'

'Oh yes.'

'You're still the guy, the one who told me he was going to be somebody, aren't you? The guy I'll do anything for when he gets back?'

She zithered her thumbnail up his zip and felt the throb behind it lurch as he groaned.

'Anything?'

'When you get back. Plus things you haven't even dreamt of. You my guy?'

'Absofuckinlutely.'

His tongue was thick and his throat dry as he spoke to the dog.

'What do you think, Bru, you want to go?'

Bru wagged his tail. Bru always wagged his tail.

'Here,' she said, 'something to keep you going.'

Nugget opened his mouth and took the tablets, but he couldn't swallow them and needed help from the bottle to get them down, one gulp for each. He put the bottle back into the bag and kissed Lynne, before leaning down to run his hand across the patch of smooth fur on Bru's head.

'Come on then, boy.'

Hints of retriever and collie dwelt beneath the overwhelming blanket of red setter, shaggy-haired and bright orange, that followed Nugget back outside. Lynne watched until the night consumed them.

Nobody commented on John Cutter holding on to the makeshift club. It wouldn't have mattered if they had; it was his. Besides, the other thing filled their minds. He held it low, in the shadow of his leg, as they left the school grounds. He wanted to inspect the blood on the branch; take pleasure from its darkening and soaking into the wood. After skirting the corner of the marsh and re-entering the town, they put distance between each other, their shameful silence compounding the space as they divided, each to their own, each to their home.

When Cutter stepped inside his house and closed the door, he was still shaking. The heavy end of the club vibrated with its own life as it swung, barely an inch from the floor. He had done a good thing. Yet nobody had thanked him. Not even a pat. He leant back against the door as he calmed. He regretted his tears, knowing that people would think he had weakened at last, that he had broken, that the boy had beaten him after all. Far from it: he had done it for her. He wanted to tell her what had happened, what he had done. He wanted her to be proud and glad. He wanted her to laugh. He could hear her telling him how brave he was, how strong. He could almost see her.

He didn't want to let go of the club, satisfying in his hand, smooth and appropriate. He walked across to his bed and sat, sinking into it. He placed the club across his knees as he stared at the central stairwell. An internal obelisk, it dominated and obstructed every domestic view.

He lifted his hand from the heavy end of the club. His

palm was tacky with the boy's blood. A bone fragment the size of a small diamond lay in the crease. He examined the point of impact, an indentation in the wood. A fingertip sat in it comfortably. He pushed, spreading the pad of his finger to fill the dent completely, forcing out a circumference thread of drying blood. He unglued his finger. What remained was an almost perfect print, the contact swirls dominant and overlaying the fine grain.

John Cutter approved.

'Guilty, John. And about time too.'

He crossed to the fire and placed the club on the mantelpiece as a fisherman would display a whale's bone, an acquired trophy from a great adventure.

Jean Ritt, 10

*Seven years earlier*

Early riser Jean Ritt, slender, bespectacled and compulsively tidy, was cleaning out Sparkle's stall in the stable. Jean was the only girl in the class who had her own pony.

Wheeling the barrow of manure across the yard, she tilted her head to one side, trying not to inhale the sickly-sweet vapours. She set the barrow down, adjusted her grip and tipped, adding Sparkle's shit to the constantly rotting mass that was warm enough to melt the snow. Returning to the stall, she took her pencil and crossed off the day on the calendar pinned to the wall. Working backwards from the coming spring, each day was numbered. The cross on this November morning meant it was only one hundred and twenty more days until she would be allowed to ride Sparkle to school again. Once the snowdrops had died and daffodils had fully established the season, she would clop through the village each weekday morning, her bobbed hair bouncing beneath her riding helmet. Just outside the gates of the school she would tether Sparkle so he could spend the day cropping fresh new grass at the edge of the marsh. At dinnertime, during those first warming weeks, some of the children, mostly girls, would rush out to feed him apples, sugar lumps and leftover scraps of their packed lunches, tentative and trying not to snatch their hands away as the pony took the offerings, his big rubbery lips tickling their palms held flat as plates in presentation.

Last spring, Sparkle had bridled at Dog Evans' extended hand. Dog had stared at the melting chocolate he had offered before throwing it hard at the pony. Sparkle reared back, jerking hard, wrong-footing Jean. Only her grip on the reins saved her from falling. Dog laughed as he pointed at Jean, attached to the skittish beast, trying to calm it. As she brought it under control, he lunged and wiped his hand down its neck, leaving a sticky brown smear. Stepping back from this small victory, he noticed the pony's growing erection. He pointed once more, drawing it to the attention of the others.

'Dirty pony,' he said.

He backed away as the other children stared at the penis.

'He's not dirty,' said Jean.

'Dirty,' Dog said before heading back to school, happy with his mischief, the pony disgraced in front of the class.

One morning soon thereafter, Jean found Sparkle bleeding from a cut to his neck. Her parents and the stable owner explained it away as an accident, even though a thorough check of the stables for nails or broken planks and the like revealed nothing. She called the police, forcing Mr Cutter to investigate. When he said Dog Evans had been in bed all night and his parents were upset that she had accused their son of harming an animal, Jean's parents had been embarrassed and made Jean feel bad. But Jenny Cutter, Jean's friend, told her that she had heard her father talking to her mother. Mr

Cutter said he could smell horse on the boy and was sure it was him had done the cutting.

By this time, persuaded by Dog, the rest of the class had found fault with Sparkle's bad breath, the flies that crawled over him, the big hairs that sprouted from his muzzle, the saliva that dripped from his bit and the regular defecation. Between classes Jean found herself alone with her pony. She would mount Sparkle, stroke his mane and sing cowboy songs to him as she walked him around the edge of the marsh. She turned him at the bottom of the driveway to the Evans' house. She no longer waved to Mrs Evans if she was there, choosing instead to look back to the school and wave to Jenny, who was always watching. Then she would walk him back to the school: over and over, Jean and Sparkle, until the bell rang, announcing the end of the dinner break.

Jean would sit next to Jenny, who would twitch her nose at the equine smell and ask her, 'How was your ride?' Jean would reply, 'Good.'

That morning Jean forked fresh hay onto the floor of Sparkle's stall and put feed in his basket. After splashing clean water into the chipped Belfast sink, she checked everything was up to her usual standard. She adjusted the calendar, quickly gave Sparkle's mane a comb and stroked his white blaze, from forehead to muzzle. Even though it was her, he quivered as she ran her fingertips over the line of the wound, halfway healed but clear in the mind.

When Jean turned the corner at Munson's newsagents an hour later, Jenny Cutter was running across the road to meet Alice Corggie. Jean could tell by the way she was moving that she was flustered. Jenny was a tall girl, gangly and uncertain, like a newborn foal.

'I ran all the way,' said Jenny. 'Sorry I'm late.'

'You're not,' said Jean. 'I'm just here myself.'

'Only a wee bit anyway,' said Alice. 'Not that it makes much difference to me.'

Jean and Jenny glanced at each other then stared at Alice, waiting. They were familiar enough with her to know not to ask. She was special enough as it was.

'I'm afraid I won't be walking with you today,' said Alice.

'Why?'

'I'm waiting for Jonny.'

Jean took a step closer to her. 'Really?'

'Yes,' said Alice. 'He's going to walk me to school.'

'He said that?'

'Yes.'

'All the way?'

'All the way.'

'Because of what Dog did yesterday?'

'Not only that.'

Jenny put the end of her ponytail in her mouth and chewed her hair while she smiled, every one of her teeth on show, unable to keep still.

'Stop that,' said Jean. 'Why are you nervous? That's what you do when you're nervous.'

'Sorry.' Jenny took the ponytail out of her mouth but kept turning it around her fingers. 'I'm not.' She took a shallow breath, 'I'm excited. You are so lucky, Alice.'

Jean nodded. 'He's gorgeous.'

There was a moment's mutual agreement before they turned as one, breathing arrested by the slushy drag of approaching feet. It was Norrie Storrie, who came around the corner, head down, blowing clouds of hot air through his fingers. The girls looked at each other and burst into a fit of giggling, their hands covering their lower faces. Norrie looked up at them and paused. Still giggling, Jean Ritt and Jenny Cutter left Alice Corggie, moving down from street light to street light towards school.

When Norrie Storrie walked past Alice with his empty delivery bag flapping, she pushed the tip of her tongue out at him. He sensed the teasing in her eyes and was blushing when he entered Munson's.

# 6

Adrenalin, amphetamine and alcohol sped through Nugget as he sat observing the house. His right leg bounced. His left knee supported his left elbow, chin in the palm of his hand as he forced the stumps of fingernails over his lower incisors, gnawing them clean. He took a sip from the bottle. The rough blend stripped another layer off his windpipe, scalded his stomach and burned along the fuse-wire of his veins to his extremities. Goosebumps crackled across his scalp like fire through stubble after harvest and his face prickled with nervous perspiration. He screwed the lid back on and bagged the bottle. Patting Bru a couple of times, he stood and they approached the dead boy's home.

His hand shook. The discoloured brass of the back door handle chattered in its casing like clockwork teeth when he gripped it.

'Fuck.'

Letting go, he glowered at his curled fingers as if they had dropped the golden apple.

He took a step back from the Evans' house and looked away. Marsh water caught the moon and the village feigned sleep. His nose ran. He wiped his sleeve across his face, snorted the slimy remains into the back of his throat and spat them onto the porch floor. The two upper panels of the door glared at him. Nugget willed himself not to think of the house as a living thing.

'Glass and timber,' he said, nodding, rocking from heel to ball, 'glass and timber.'

He scooped the half-bottle from the mailbag. He sucked a mouthful out, then another. He took a breath, held it, released it slowly. Stepping forward, he finger-tipped the handle. His touch was steady. He grasped, turned and pushed in one withheld breath. The door stopped after a few inches and he collided with it comic-book style, the slapstick impact splitting the skin above his eye. He straightened himself quickly as he surveyed for anybody who might have seen. It was quiet and still. A barn owl ghosted by. Bru was motionless.

Exploring the cut, his fingertips came away wet, and he could feel the wetness trickling through his eyebrow.

'Shit. Nugget, come on, get a grip, man.'

Bru whined.

'Shh, boy, keep that down.' He crouched and held the dog's head in his hands, his blood streaking its fur. 'You don't want them all to hear, do you? Don't you want your share? Steak every day; think about that. All for a little shush. Steak every day, my goodness, sounds good to me.'

Untangling a used handkerchief from his pocket, he applied pressure to the wound as he pushed against the door again, using his scrawny body to steadily increase the force. There was some give before it stopped once more.

'What's your thoughts, Bru, winter damp?'

With the door partially open, he edged his head into the gap to try and see inside, but snapped back as he in-haled the interior smells that seeped out. The rank cloud of bad air wrapped itself around him and slammed him against the wall as he gagged at the stench of butchery and cooking, or maybe rendering. Bru hunkered down behind his master's heels and laid his head on his front paws. Nugget pushed himself off the wall, shook his head to clear it.

'Come on, boy, let's get this thing done; go home rich.'

When he thought he could handle the smell, he took a few steps back before throwing himself at the door. He shouldered it open enough to be able to get in, scuffing a rough rainbow into the grain of the floor. He saw it was wedged on paper. Hovering between moonlight and the interior, he peered in, trying to make sense of the room. Taking his head torch from his pocket, he turned it on and held it high. It lit upon a flotilla of tiny origami boats in a column about a foot wide, sailing away from him across the floor towards the pale light of the rear window. Bending down to pick one up, he realised it was currency, crisp and clean. The boats were banknotes, identically folded and carefully positioned.

Strapping the torch on, Nugget used the handles for support and swung into the room. He was still holding onto the handles when he saw that Bru had stayed outside, framed in the tall slit of partial doorway.

'Come on, boy.' Nugget crooked his finger, calling the dog. The dog leant forward. 'That's it, good boy, come on.' Bru crept in, head low and tail down.

Once inside, Nugget saw that the boats halved the room, passing beneath a small coffee table, one of the dining chairs and over an upturned box, straight as a Roman road, determined as a cockroach migration. To the right of the line was what he took to be the living area. A large sofa and leather armchair faced an open fireplace, embers still glowing in the hearth. To the left, the dining area, a table and chairs, next to what he remembered as being the kitchen.

Fascination popped the torchlight around the room without method, erratic as the speeding thoughts in Nugget's head. It wasn't dirty, as the smell had suggested. Although it was a world created without recent adult guidance, a kind of order was in place. But the manner of things gave a sense of the awful. Animal traps, both gins and snares, against the back wall. Pelts draped over the sofa gave it the look of a sleeping bear. Worst of all were the skeletal remains. Piled in the space beneath the stairs on the far wall, chalk collections with the look of both ossuary and shrine; the charnel-house contents of some other way of life – size-graded cairns of skulls, limbs, ribcages, the awkward shapes of pelvis and scapula; the tiny disassociated links of the tails, feet and spinal columns of all manner and size of beast.

'Jesus.'

He covered his eyes against it but still saw the retinal print of what he had found. Turning away, he opened his eyes to journey with the boats toward the wan square of the far window, to be somewhere else. As he became accustomed to the surroundings, his attention returned to the boats.

'Just look at all that fucking money, Bru. It's why we're here, boy. And there's more, lots more.'

He held some of the notes to Bru's muzzle.

'I don't know why I waited for him to be gone. Every

time I delivered one of those little fat envelopes I knew I needed it more than he did. I know for a fact that these paper fucking boats are only part of my treasure. Let's find it. Search, Bru. Pieces of steak, pieces of steak.'

Nugget knew the boy had never bought anything with the money. On the rare occasion he had been seen in the village, he was avoided but watched. After his first ill-fated attempt to buy clothes, he'd never again stepped into a shop. 'We don't stock your size,' Mac the tailor had told him. 'It'll be years until we do.' He'd been bundled out, unaware that every junior-sized item of clothing had been removed from the store, too painful a reminder, and sent overseas through the auspices of Father Finnegan and his church. For a while, women's clothes disappeared from washing lines and reappeared on the boy, including a T-shirt of Lynne's. Nobody demanded or wanted them back. This stopped when clothes they had seen Shep wear came to fit him. The one display along Main Street that had attracted him back into town was the bookshop. He would look at the books the way others would watch a bank of televisions, transported, as though imagining the lives and journeys within each volume. It struck Nugget as strange that he never tried to buy one. They all knew he could read. He scanned the room for a bookshelf, concentrating, chewing his lip.

He stopped.

'Christ, Nugget.'

He slapped himself across the forehead, knocking his torch to the floor.

'Books?' he said, focusing the light before refitting it. 'We're not here for books. Come on, Bru.'

His mission back on track, he proceeded to ransack the place, pulling drawers open, smacking cupboard doors back on their hinges and flipping the lids off any boxes he found. Nothing.

'Lynne's right, Bru.' His breathing was shallow and rapid. 'I was stupid for leaving it this long. I don't know what I'll do if someone else has got to it first. Every delivery was an investment. That's what I'd tell her. Well, Nugget's here to withdraw.'

The circle of his searchlight flashed across the wall, stopped and backtracked. On the mantelpiece was a neat pyramid of packages, offset like brickwork, their placing so uniformly precise that they had looked to be part of the fireplace surround, an intricate carving, the peak of which obscured a small section of the mirror that hung above the fire. Nugget cooed.

He ran his hands down the sides of the money mound. He was gentle with the unopened packets. Something halfway between a sob and a whimper escaped from him. For the second time that night, his cock pushed against his trousers. He looked into the mirror, euphoric and amphetamine-stiffened. The three gold teeth that gave him his name, two incisors and a canine, shone in the torch beam. He yanked his zip down and pulled his erection out, tugging until jism sizzled on the embers. His scrotum hung soft and warm in the updraught as he subsided. The base of his shaft rubbed against the nylon zipper of his work-issue trousers as he teased the final drops out, sliming over his fingers as he pushed it back in. He began to weep. His nose ran. He wiped his hand across it but only succeeded in swapping snot for salty ejaculate. Forced into his nose, the smell was even stronger than that of the house. His innards lurched. He leant against the mirror.

A glimmer behind him caught his attention. It came from the bottom of the largest mound of bones. Low in the reflection he saw the ivory dome of a human skull. He vomited, sluicing his nostrils with whisky and bile, spraying the sleeping bear. The acid boiled in his windpipe. Sweat iced his body as he hunched over, leaning on his knees, spitting. When he could stand, he used the strength remaining in his shaking frame to scoop the packets of money into his postbag. He closed the flap and embraced them.

He shivered as he stooped to inspect the skull. He wondered if it had been the starting point, the foundation; if the rest of the skeleton was at the bottom of each pile. A silver chain was threaded through both eye sockets, wrapped a couple of times around the ridge of bone that separated them. The large crucifix attached to the chain leant against the skull, partially occluding one of the sockets. Nugget moved the cross to reveal an irregular dent in the forehead. Hairline cracks radiated from it in all directions. He shook with wheezy laughter.

'So that's where you got to, you fucking mad bastard.' He knelt. 'Father Finnegan – Fireball Finnegan. Just look at you. Here all the time. Jesus. And the company you're keeping.'

He lifted the crucifix and wiped it. It was heavy, solid silver. It wouldn't fit through the eye socket and he couldn't find the end of the chain, so he tried easing it free with gentle pulling. When the whole pile of bones shifted, he started and dropped it, his breath arrested, waiting for the collapse. Bru backed away, growling.

'It's okay, boy. It's okay.' He dragged the dog close with the hand not holding onto the money. 'It would only have been a bonus anyway, and hard to sell. We've got what we came for. We'll take the boats. He can keep it.'

He managed a grin as he sat back, able to relax with the skull now he knew who it was.

'Seems like yesterday, seeing that cross again. The fucking trouble you caused. You fucked with this village more than anything else, you know that? Poor Mary, she still thinks you're coming back. Can you believe that? She wrote to the Pope asking where you'd been sent. No reply. She had a baby boy; he's got your hair.' Nugget made the sign of the cross. 'Bless me, Father, for I have sinned; but not as much as you did.' He stood and backed away from the priest's skull. 'You look better without the moustache, though, I'll grant you that.'

He poured whisky into his mouth and rinsed it around until the burning of his gums took his mind off the taste of the vomit. He crossed the line of boats and spat into the fire. Whoosh. Embers ignited the fumes and Bru barked at the violent flare as the whole room momentarily lit up.

'Hush now,' Nugget said, staring down his almost concave chest to his stomach. 'Bru, that's enough. No more. You hear me?'

Strings of puke and bile on his jacket had glistened in the light from the fireball. He felt soiled. He needed to wash his hands.

He entered the kitchen looking for the sink and stopped. A rust-coloured fox fur was spread across the wooden draining board. Bloody water drained into the enamel sink. A stockpot sat on the wood-burning stove. He shuddered as he reached out and touched the lid. The pot and the stove were cold. He couldn't bring himself to look inside; didn't want to be confronted with the head, the skeleton, the whole body, meat and all, whatever was in there. Bru brushed against his legs, going further into the room, and he heard the dog licking.

'What you got, boy?' he said, glancing down. As he did, his light passed over Bru onto the redness on the floor and his legs gave way.

Bru was licking his face when he came to.

He pushed him away, wiping his face hard against the taste of ripening flesh on his lips. But Bru came back.

'No.'

He pushed the dog again and followed it with a two-footed kick that sent him sliding back across the kitchen floor into the skinned carcass of the fox, stretched out on sacking on the floor, muscle and sinew exposed, white teeth bared in a perpetual snarl, a big chunk of the hind-quarter eaten away.

'No, I said. Stay away from me, Bru. Just stay away.'

A protruding fox eye reflected jade green. Bru whined and edged forward, brushing the floor with his tail as he followed Nugget, keeping his distance as his master dragged himself out of the room.

Nugget couldn't look at the dog as he sat leaning against the staircase.

The banister was sticky. Like the chair and the dining table, it was stained with an unholy patina, as if the juice of the boy had seeped into the furniture, stained the floorboards and nourished the whole building with his containment. Nugget used the wall for support as he made his way up the stairs.

The state of the bathroom on the half-landing surprised him. He'd expected the smell to make his eyes water, tidemarks around the bath, and for the toilet to be brown with use. It was clean. He didn't even stop Bru drinking from the bowl.

'At least it'll take some of the fox off.'

Before Bru knew anything about it, Nugget had grabbed his collar and held his head down while he flushed the chain. Bru's bark spluttered as the water cascaded about him and Nugget attacked his stained muzzle, rubbing water through his teeth and over his fur as he cleaned him. The thought of the dog licking his face made his innards buckle again, forcing viscous yellow dregs up into his mouth. He spat them into the sink as Bru shook himself dry. Swilling the bile down the drain with the traces of vomit and fox flesh he'd soaped off his hands, he felt weak and light-headed, as if he was ridding himself of strength. He dried his hands and threw the rough towel into the bath before leaving.

Standing on the half-landing, he glanced up into the darkness of the top floor.

Those that had to pass the church on the way home had. Nobody was waiting to confess. Wittin kicked the baptismal font.

'They could all go to prison,' he said. 'On my word, the whole lot of them. And they deserve to.'

His words echoed for a moment, sounding silly and as empty as the church.

He heard the latch of the door as it was lifted. Mary Magnal entered the church.

'Mary.'

'Father.'

'What can I do for you?'

'I'd like you to hear my confession.'

'Of course.'

Inside the confessional, he waited for Mary to be ready. Sounds he was familiar with, having heard many tiresome confessions from the woman already. She did the annoying small sigh thing she always did before she started.

'Bless me, Father, for I have sinned. It has been—'

'I know, Mary. It was this morning. Less than a day has passed.'

'But the day has contained sin, Father.'

'Indeed. Please, continue.'

'Father, I committed an act of violence. I struck a priest.'

'Okay.' He waited. 'And?'

'And?'

'Is there anything else, Mary? Anything you feel you may need God's forgiveness for?'

A small sigh before, 'I took pleasure from the death of another.'

'Mary, you did more than that.' Wittin put his face against the grille, close to the woman's. 'What happened tonight was wrong.'

'No.'

'I'm sorry? It was a sin.'

'What happened tonight was right.'

'Mary, have you heard yourself?'

'I took pleasure from it. I take pleasure from it. It will be my eternal sin.'

Wittin groaned as he sat back.

'Mary, you're the truest Christian soldier in the village. If I don't have you, whom do I have? We could do the right thing, by God, by the church, by the boy you buried.'

'You would do more harm than good.'

'But to say nothing is to go to hell. We could lead the way, you and I.'

'John Cutter led the way,' she said. 'You could follow.'

'Mary, thou shalt not kill.'

He listened to the sounds of Mary Magnal preparing to leave.

Jenny Cutter, 10

*Seven years earlier*

'Do you think Alice and Jonny have kissed?' said Jean, the moment she thought they were out of Alice's earshot.

'No,' said Jenny, 'don't be silly, he's …' She stopped and looked down at Jean. 'Do you?'

'I think so.'

Jenny looked anxious. 'But you don't know?' She put her ponytail in her mouth.

'Stop it.' Jean flicked the hair away. Jenny flinched, contracting, as if in anticipation of a further commotion. 'I'm sorry,' said Jean, quickly. She took Jenny's hand. 'I'm sorry, I didn't mean to.'

Jean was always telling Jenny off for chewing the ends of her hair. Mrs Cutter chewed her hair all the time. What Jean didn't know was that sometimes it was the only thing that stopped Mrs Cutter crying.

'It's okay, I'm sorry.'

'Jenny, what for?'

'For not being happy for Alice any more.'

'But why?'

'She's too young.' Jenny's face creased with concern. 'I'm scared for her.'

'Scared?'

'What if her dad finds out? Do you think he'll be

angry? He will, won't he? We can't say anything, if we see him.'

'Jenny, slow down. I don't know what you mean.'

Jenny Cutter worried her hair around the fingers of her free hand as she studied the snowflakes building up on her coat sleeve.

'My dad would be angry. I just know it.'

'Mr Corggie's different.'

'You think so? Because he's a doctor?'

'No, because he's different. And anyway, even if they do kiss, that's okay, isn't it? It's not … you know.'

'The other thing.'

'Yes.'

'That would make Mr Corggie angry, I'll bet.'

'That would make any daddy angry.'

The two girls looked at each other. Jean smiled and Jenny responded.

'You okay?'

'Yes.'

Jean took Jenny's hand. Jenny had something of the rag-dolly about her, twig-limbed, loose-jointed and small of waist, as ready to be picked up and held as dangled or thrown.

'Where are your new boots?' asked Jean. 'I've only just noticed.'

Jenny favoured chunky footwear that anchored her and looked like it stopped her spindly frame from blowing away. Looking down at her slip-ons, well broken in and daily polished, she shook her head.

'I decided to save them.'

'For best?'

Jenny shrugged.

'Jenny.'

A few seconds passed.

'Calvin laughed at them. He made me not like them any more. I told my mum they were a bit sore. She said I should wear them around the house until I break them in.'

'Jenny, why do you care what Calvin thinks? He's stupid and fat.'

'I don't, not really.'

'You should tell him then.'

'I know. I will.'

Jenny knew swear words, proper ones, those associated with craftsmen and criminals, and had mastered how to use them. Most of the boys had been their targets. Most of the boys had at some point laughed at her. The only one who didn't find her amusing was Dog Evans. He never laughed and he didn't scare Jenny Cutter.

The only person who scared Jenny was her father, Police Officer John Cutter. He'd never laid a hand on her, but he ruled their home with the threat of the back of it.

He hadn't frowned or scowled or passed comment. But John Cutter didn't say anything nice about Jenny's new boots when she left for school the previous morning. He said nothing when she returned home. He cleaned them and gave them their first polish and left them on the stairs for her to take up when she went to her bed. But Jenny could hear them, his words from the shopping trip to the city, a trip he always hated and ruined for Jenny and her mother. 'Unsuitable ... poorly manufactured

66

... impractical for the winter ... they wouldn't last five minutes ... expensive ...' All delivered as sound advice from one who knew, in the reasonable yet joyless tone that was already anticipating 'I told you so'.

Jenny had loved her mum for insisting she got the boots, for telling her that once in a while pretty was enough; men didn't understand this. Her father shook his head, handed over the money and walked away while her mum paid. He was silent throughout the journey home. Sitting behind him, Jenny had taken the boots off as quietly as she could and put them back in their box.

Officer Cutter kept the law when he needed to. At home, he laid the law down because he could. Jenny sensed the time would come when she would become another disappointment to him. She didn't want to be like her mum, floating around the house like a golden ghost, wondering what to do next apart from look pretty. Aside from Mrs Evans, Jenny knew she was her mum's only friend. When her dad wasn't there, they talked. When Jenny was alone, she used his tools. The first time John and Deborah Cutter saw the small crescent shapes of a carpenter's chisel cut into the top of Jenny's thigh was the afternoon they identified her body.

'Come on,' said Jean. 'Let's go and tell Calvin what we think of him. Then we can look after Connor. He'll need a cuddle in all this cold.'

'That sounds good,' said Jenny.

She linked arms with Jean and they glanced back up the street to where Alice still stood in the light of Munson's waiting for Jonny Raffique.

# 7

Deborah Cutter took the wheelbarrow leaning against the wall of the house, figuring nobody would be using it tonight, telling herself she'd return it when she was finished. Avoiding the streets, she pushed it along the paths and lanes of the village, through puddles and past bins, until she rounded the back of the fire station. As usual, it was unmanned and unlocked.

In the gloomy chill of the station house, she opened the appliance door and climbed into the cab she had once been fucked in. She took a torch from the shoulder strap of a breathing apparatus set, then searched station cupboards and cubbyholes until she found what she was looking for: a five-gallon jerry can and a length of hose.

She sucked on the end of the tube to draw fuel from the tank. She pushed it into the open can and listened to the hollow metallic splashing, gradually dulling as the container filled. When the diesel gushed over the brim, she pulled the tube out and screwed the lid on, her coated fingers slipping off as it tightened. She pulled her cuff down over her hand to give her enough purchase to finish the job, before dragging the can to the wicket gate in the back door and heaving it out. As she stepped out of the station house and closed the gate behind her, red diesel continued to bleed over the scrubbed tiled floor, coursing through tyre treads and seeping into mortar cracks.

Alice Corggie, 11

*Seven years earlier*

Alice Corggie sheltered from the snow beneath the striped canvas awning of Munson's, backlit by the lights from the shop window and the sparkling glass jars of boiled sweets in rows. She was yearning for Jonny, her new protector. They came from different sides of the town but they both had to walk down Main Street to get to the school.

'Good morning, Alice,' said Ed Munson, standing in the door of his shop. He put a partially smoked cigar to his mouth, held his lighter to it and drew.

'Morning, Mr Munson,' said Alice.

He opened his mouth and a lazy cloud of blue-grey cigar smoke drifted out. Alice watched it turn and roll in the air until it reached her.

'I like that smell,' she said. 'It's nice.'

'Mm, me too.'

'It reminds me of my dad.'

'Same cigar right enough.' He held his cigar out to her, teasing. 'You want a shot?'

Ed Munson was quick to withdraw the offer when Alice went to take the cigar.

'You wee bugger.'

She gave him her best roguish smile and a stare of

such assured depth that she saw he was almost disarmed.

'You need to be keeping your eye on me.'

'So I see,' he said.

And he did. She could feel him watching as she turned her attention to the street.

'You see Norrie?'

'He is so weird,' said Alice.

'How so?'

'Birdwatching?'

'Boys have hobbies; birdwatching is his.'

'But he's obsessed.'

'No, he's paying attention to the world about him, Alice. He sees things, notices.' Ed Munson glanced down at the young girl of Norrie's dreams. 'I'd say that was a fine quality, wouldn't you?'

'I suppose.' Alice was distracted, checking the street.

'So,' he said, 'Jean and Jenny making you wait today?'

Alice shook her head. 'I'm waiting on Jonny.'

Ed Munson drew on his cigar again, holding the flavour for a few seconds before releasing for her to share.

'Jonny, is it?'

He looked down at her and raised his eyebrows, envious of the boy Raffique. Alice was pleased with his response.

'Lucky him. He seems a nice boy.'

'That's why I chose him.'

'Oh, you chose him, did you?'

'Of course.'

'He didn't take pity on you?'

'Mum says you should never pity the pretty because they'll inherit whoever they choose.'

'Well, your mum should know. She's a beauty herself.'

'The most beautiful woman in the village.'

'That's your dad speaking.'

'And Mum.'

'And what else does your mum tell you?'

'That I'll make grown men wish they were young again.'

She looked up at Ed Munson as he coughed and spluttered over his cigar.

'Go down the wrong way?'

Munson nodded, wiping his mouth.

'Want me to pat your back?'

'No, no thank you,' he said, recovering. 'I'm fine. I should be getting back to work.'

'Okay.'

'You make sure young Jonny's good to you, mind.'

'I will.'

Ed Munson went back inside, to newspapers, cigarettes and sweets.

Juan 'Jonny' Raffique was still considered new to the school. He was the most exotic thing Alice had ever seen or could imagine. Black-haired and dark-skinned, he had arrived unannounced one morning with his mother, Tina Louise. As impossible as it seemed to the gawking, pale-skinned class, they had come all the way from America and now lived in the squat three-roomed gatehouse at the entrance of the Struans' driveway. That Monday, every child had been transfixed. Jonny was an alien deity. Nearly all the girls fell in love with him. (Lucy Magnal didn't love anybody.) The boys were completely wrong-footed by his appearance and unsure how to react. They splashed around in their combined juices of envy and admiration as his Californian accent turned every word into magic.

Alice fell headlong for Jonny the instant she heard him speak. As he introduced himself, standing at the front of the classroom, the sea-washed syllables of his hometown, Sausalito, swelled from his throat and poured from his mouth as *saucealeedo*, a gorgeous, sun-drenched liquid. It made her giddy and dizzy, moist and warm. When the teacher told him to take the vacant seat next to Alice, a seat too hot for any other boy, she was rendered inarticulate and clumsy by his words. Jonny Raffique's voice was Alice's first sexual experience.

From that moment, Alice Corggie loved Jonny Raffique and didn't care who knew. She bound her initials with his inside countless naively skewered hearts, on desktops, exercise books and, in one unseen declaration, on the breast flesh sprouting within her blouse: a juvenile tattoo of red and blue biro that would never wash off because she drew it the night before she died. Now she waited outside Munson's, desperate to show him.

Alice would have been his first victim.

Jonny would have been her only mistake.

# 8

The boy's bed was stripped. The arm of a ragged cotton pyjama jacket hung from within the folds of the blankets, sheets and pillowcases pushed into a plastic laundry basket in the corner. The tallboy wardrobe behind the door was all but empty, containing a couple of changes of clothes at most. The wall held one empty picture hook and an old mirror put beyond any practical use by damp. Nugget turned the knob of an old-fashioned radio. It was dead. The low wooden shelves at the footboard held no toys and few books. He recognised the books from his own child's schooling and instinctively picked them up. They were well used; thumbed, folded and worn. Especially the bottle-green hardbacks of the *Children's World Encyclopedia*, which Nugget knew contained somewhere within its pages instructions on how to fold a sheet of paper into a boat. When he lifted them to his nose, he was disturbed to find that they still held the smell of the classroom, and the day Norrie died came rushing back. He threw them down.

On the other side of the room, the rolltop writing bureau and its attendant swivel chair shone from regular cleaning. Nugget wheeled the chair out and sat down, resting the mailbag of money on his lap. Expecting the desk to be locked, he was surprised by the easy sliding motion of the shutter as it opened up.

*Get the chimney swept.*
*Buy clothes for the winter.*
*Make sure you pay the bills.*

Apart from a few pencils, a jotter, some drawing pins and a musty smell, all the bureau contained was a collection of these notes, lying on the writing surface, each signed with an S.

*We hope you're looking after yourself.*
*Make sure you stay well fed.*
*Are you keeping the house clean?*
*Your mother says hello.*

Until Nugget got to the bottom one, sellotaped to the leather.

*Hope to see you soon.*

The first one?

'Hope.' He sighed and replaced the notes, trying to keep them in their original order. 'What a fucking word.'

He switched his head torch off and stared across at the bed next to the window.

The icy blue moonlight emphasised the desperate emptiness of the room; without comfort of any form. All the boy did was sleep here. The net curtain wafted away from the broken pane, through which Nugget glimpsed the ghostly school ruins where shy of an hour ago they had buried him.

Bru jumped up onto the bed and lay down.

'May as well make yourself comfortable,' Nugget said, pushing away from the bureau and rising from the chair. He shouldered the money as he walked across and sat next to Bru, his back to the window. The dog looked to be taking his advice, relaxing into his usual sleeping position. Nugget stroked the soft dip between the animal's hackles as he wondered what was behind the white-gloss door across the landing.

'Stay, boy.'

He turned his torch back on and partially opened the door. He poked his head around as if expecting somebody to be inside. It was empty. The parents' bedroom. It looked untouched. Although damp, it was spotlessly clean. When Nugget picked the single framed photograph up from the dressing table, he saw it had been dusted. The surfaces and the mirror had been wiped recently. The sheets and cover on the bed were laundered. A seasonal branch of berry-laden holly stuck out of a small vase. He lifted it. It had water in it. The room was a shrine.

'No fucking way. You really thought they were coming back.' He hugged the bag of money hard, then sagged into the bed as the boy's loneliness dawned on him and connected them both. 'Oh Jesus. You sorry little fucker.'

Looking at the picture of Shep and Rebecca Evans deepened his mood. Delving through the envelopes of money, he retrieved the bottle and drained the contents into his freshly emptied stomach. The whisky dropped through him like molten lead and scorched its way straight to his head. They were young in the picture, smiling as they leaned against their new car. Nice clothes as well, fashionable and fitted. Must have been from the days when they were doing well, before *he* came along. Then Nugget noticed that it was more than a hug that he was giving her. Shep had his hand on her tummy, which meant that it must have been taken after they'd moved here.

He'd liked Shep the moment they met. Most people had been inclined to. It was obvious that the man had a good streak in him. Unlike many others, Nugget had also liked Rebecca, and would have considered her time well spent had she ever succumbed to any of the advances he'd made when Shep was away on business. He'd made it plain he thought she was too good for this end-of-the-road, nowhere village. Only the child held her back, and, in the eyes of the villagers, proved him wrong. He'd persisted until the accident and the priest had put her well and truly out of bounds.

Nugget leant over to the dressing table. He rummaged through the drawers. Some papers, some photographs, a birth certificate with the boy's real name on it. In the middle drawer, nothing but the stump of a black eyeliner and a pink handkerchief with an R embroidered into the corner. It was still fragrant. It didn't belong to this house. He put his nose into the drawer. He could smell her. He was erect again.

He pumped a few pearly dribbles onto the cotton hanky.

He sucked the final drops of whisky from the neck. He didn't want to leave. He was growing fond of this room. He lay on her pillow as the insanity of the house spun around him. He fell asleep clutching the mailbag.

Juan 'Jonny' Raffique, 11

*Seven years earlier*

Tina Louise and Jonny Raffique shivered as they opened the door on the morning. Snowflakes fell through the light of the twin gateway lamps outside their new home.

'You think it will ever stop?'

He shrugged. 'I kinda like it.'

'You are a liar,' she said, 'and a bad one at that.'

'Just trying to make it work, Mom.'

'I know.'

She looked down at him. Handsome as he was, his sallow face and brown eyes were haunted by the fact that they had been forced into flight, across the ocean.

'We'll make it work, don't worry.'

He never let on that the village felt like the end of the world. He felt cold and damp every morning he awoke.

'How many hours of daylight today, Mom?'

'Six, I guess, maybe less.'

'That's something.'

'Hey you, be positive.'

She gave him a hug, which he returned.

'Love you, Mom.'

Jonny Raffique kissed Tina Louise, pulled his hood up and stepped out into the snow. At the gate, he waved to his mom, zipped up his parka so that his face all but disappeared, then hid his hands in the high side-pockets and pulled it tight around his body. It was the thickest, heaviest item of clothing he had ever owned, but it couldn't keep him warm.

# 9

Deborah surrendered to the weight of the wheelbarrow. Joints reconnected and her breathing recovered as her heart battered inside the straitjacket of arms bound around herself.

Why was the door open? She stared into the dead boy's house from the foot of its porch steps. Her lower jaw hung, her lungs pumped, her tongue dried into the base of her mouth. Her hair was lank with grease. Droplets trickled down her spine-line. Did he know nobody would go in, or that he wasn't coming back? Did he go out there to die? She shuddered, instantly back in the school ruins. The sight of him sticking out of the ground was a white spike in her memory. It was driven in deep, a lightning rod to the root of the pain that tore through time and brought Jenny back to life. Tonight the hurt had been renewed. Deborah was appalled with herself. She had spoken to him: 'Why are you here?' But he had made her do it, just by being there. She'd cried, given herself away. He had no right to be there, to look to her for help. It was unfair. It was an unjust union. The horror of it had sheared sense and strength from her mind.

Nervy and jelly-legged, she heaved the can up the steps. It bounced against her shins. Muscles, sinews and ligaments chorused resistance as they were forced back into use. Determination drove her dehydrated body. She was satisfied when she placed the can on the step; sickened as she tasted the smell from inside the house. It reached into her. She sealed her mouth and pinched her nose tight, breathing from her palm as though it held the last remaining scoop of fresh air. Her raggybit pinky nail dug into the pearled blister caused by the hot candle wax of the vigil mass. The blister tore easily, humour bleeding across knuckles that had whitened as the boy's skull had been crushed, through the criss-cross diamonds of age etched on unwashed skin.

When she was ready, she opened her eyes and loosened her hand. What she saw confused her. Paper boats, grounded, facing in the same direction, triangles of expectation, queuing to leave. They pointed towards the back window. Moonbeams fell on the leading boats. Deborah saw ascension, escape.

'Why didn't you just go?'

She slapped herself.

'Shame on you, Debbie Cutter.'

Pushing a rat tail of hair into her mouth, she ground the filaments hard between her teeth, refusing to cry again.

Deborah had ended up on the opposite side of the glade from John Cutter, her vigil flame right up to her face, wanting him to see her, to look at her. She couldn't remember the last time they had spoken, but she could recall every crease of his face. She no longer prayed for her John to return, but she still hoped. He stood back, his face hidden. She had watched his active hands as they worked, wringing – craving use. But instead of John, it was the self-buried boy between them who had looked back and understood. Every 'no' she had ever felt screamed through her. She looked beyond him, searching for John. She saw his hands part and was convinced he had seen her, that saving her was the impetus for his steady walk from under the trees, his easy bend to pick up the stray branch, his raising of strong arms and their swift release. She had wanted to cry out, to cheer. He had done it for her. But she was dumbfounded. Her big strong John broke like a dam. She had only seen him cry once before.

They helped him, held him while he wept, kept her away, as though shielding him, keeping infection away from a wound. Even later, when the spade had been pushed towards her, its holder, Sandy Blades, couldn't look at her.

Why didn't they help her? Why hadn't anybody ever helped her? She was empty. She needed to be full. She had needed their seed. Why hadn't they ever seen that, any of them? She'd been drunk and fucked so often that the misuses were a blur. Rare moments of laughter stood out – especially the last one, after hours, on the bonnet of a car at the back of the tavern. The barman had been swaying as he joked about her being slack. She'd ridiculed him for being limp; sniggering as she flicked his 'little boy's willy' away from her, comparing him with others she'd had before losing control, hysterical as he tried to force it back in. She laughed until he hit her. He hit her more than once. No longer limp, he flipped her over and tore her anus, beer slopping from his bottle onto her lower back.

Deborah cried herself to sleep behind the tavern; her

pants stuck to her, her face turning purple, her arm as a pillow.

As the sun rose, she felt her hair being brushed off her face, gently, but still enough to wake her. Struggling to focus, she was briefly hypnotised by the light refracting through the dewdrops suspended on the wool of her jumper. Gradually, within the birdsong of the dawn chorus, she recognised the slow exhalations of someone close by, watching. Blinking, she moved her head to see. Above her stood a child in a white dress, radiant with sunlight and long blonde hair.

'Hello.'

'Hello, Sabbath,' said Deborah.

'It's good you know my name.'

'I guess so.'

'No need to waste time on introductions.'

Sabbath held her hand out. She kept her slender fingers straight and still as Deborah took hold. Slight as the child was, Deborah took strength from her as she pulled herself into a half-sitting position.

'We need to go,' said Sabbath.

She gave a gentle tug, but Deborah resisted. She was tender and it hurt to move and she remembered what had happened the night before. She wiped young tears away before they had time to fall.

'Be strong for Sabbath.'

'I can't, I'm sore.'

'You need to be strong.'

Sabbath tugged again, coaxing. After a few seconds, Deborah allowed the child to pull her up. She winced, feeling raw and ripped.

'He used the wrong hole.'

'I know,' said Sabbath.

'Why?'

'He doesn't care about you.'

Deborah looked down at Sabbath.

'Do you?'

'Of course.' Sabbath took Deborah's hands in her own. 'Why else would I be here?'

'I'm glad,' said Deborah. 'It's nice. I feel better with you here.'

'Shall we?'

Sabbath led the way with faltering steps. Slow progress saw them emerge from behind the tavern on to the footpath. No traffic passed them as they walked home together, Deborah holding on to the child.

Sabbath still had hold when Deborah was clean and she fell asleep.

The girl was right. The barman didn't care. He had a story and he was happy to tell those who would listen. It started another wave of derision and condemnation. It also teased some of them back to her, bottle in hand by way of payment. Past beaux who had wearied of her guiding hands, fat men with no hope, young men with no experience. Yet not a man in the village who wanted to use her wrongly could meet her gaze. It was over. She rejected them all. Some of them had stood in the circle around the dead boy. One of them passed her the spade.

Deborah tore the skin off her blister, nails digging into the subcutaneous flesh to feel the pain, refusing to indulge in pity. It helped clear her mind to the now, to this act of cleansing herself of everything Dog Evans. She sat the jerrycan on the top step of the Evans' house. She pushed down and turned the sprung cap until it popped off. She positioned the mouth to pour into the house and tilted it.

She watched as the diesel glugged, rippling with indigo moonlight as it spread. The boats became animated, lifted from the floor by the incoming tide to set sail and float away from her on the swell. She envied them. She emptied the can.

The disposable plastic lighter was warm from her jeans pocket. The liquid visible through its clear walls was precious, the answer to her prayers. She sensed an end and was surprised to hear herself snigger as she held the flame to the spilled fuel. It went out. Her thumb re-spun the wheel against the flint. It sparked and caught. She held the lighter to the floor, concentrating to keep it in the thin layer of fume as the heat of the flame transferred to the metal collar and into the pad of her thumb. She held it in place until the diesel caught, sucking air into the house as the multicoloured ignition coiled away across the room to the window. She let go. The lighter dropped through the spreading sheet of flame. She watched as each boat ignited individually in the aurora of burning fumes: brief fireworks on a shallow sea. It was only in the moment of their burning that she realised they were banknotes.

Pushing away from the door, Deborah slumped against the wooden upright that supported the porch and faced back into the house. She was exhausted. She watched as the smoke thickened. Feathers of flame flew up table, chairs and armchairs. Fire spread to the walls and soon the fabric of the house was alight. Her thumb pulsed with the pain of another developing blister. She tried to wipe the burn into her Levis, rubbing it against the frayed leg seam. They'd been good to her for over a decade, been well used. At times, this faded pair of jeans was all she could rely on. A smile creased her cheeks as she gazed, fascinated, into the warp and weft of the denim that flickered with the killing of the house.

# IO

It was a large room, occupying the whole ground floor. When the newly married John Cutter had finished his work and allowed people in to see, their neighbours had marvelled at the open-plan design. It was audacious, bright and airy, space for the soul and ventilation for the eyes. It made people smile and yelled freedom. The freedom had been playful. At first John and Debbie had played alone. Then came Jenny. Jenny Cutter had crawled, toddled, cycled and roller-skated around the central column of the stairwell that appeared to hold the rest of the home up like Atlas held the heavens. The floor retained the arcs of roller-wheel marks.

John Cutter mourned the room's lack of use. It had been years since the solid wood counter he had spanned the right-hand wall with was busy with family activity. Food had been prepared as Play-Doh had been rolled and squeezed or crayons pushed across the back of old wallpaper. Meals had been cooked. Plans had been made. A future had been expected. The dining table was not set. What was visible of his workbench below the far window was dusty and unused. Beside the open fireplace, a solid single bed dominated the left-hand side of the room. It was a blunt frame of spars and beams, jointed and pegged, made for sleep and nothing else. After finishing his bed, he had retired his carpenter's tools. Save for a single gouge, they dressed one side of the stairwell's outer wall. Civilian clothes hung from the other. The narrow back wall held his police uniform.

He crossed from the fireplace to the concealed stairway and pulled the heavy velvet drape aside. The smell that fell into the room came from a distant past. It was the smell of more than one: of talcum powder, flowers and clean clothes. From the bottom of the stairwell Cutter looked up into the gloom. He couldn't recall the last time he'd climbed the stairs. His left hand encircling the ceramic ball that weighted the pull string, he applied steady pressure, as if to a trigger. The mechanism clicked and the light bulb popped. In the brief flash he saw that Jenny's bedroom door was open, that wallpaper was peeling away at the top of the stairs, a rainwater stain ran through the ceiling rose and a nest of cobwebs gave the impression they held the light in place. The darkness that followed the snapshot was solid and disappointing.

He sighed.

Rooting through the cupboard beneath the stairs, John Cutter found a bulb. He took the small black Maglite off its hook. He slid his overcoat off and hung it up. He noticed the wet stains down the back and in the armpits. Unhooking it, he draped it over the radiator and turned the valve to allow hot water to flow through.

On the landing, he changed the bulb, the torch held in his teeth. The bulb flared as soon as he screwed it in. Looking down, he blinked until he was used to the light. He saw his footprints on the stairs. If dust consisted mostly of human skin, how could the layer on the stairs could be so thick?

Their bedroom door was still closed. Two steel brackets with security screws ensured that it would remain so. Behind it was an almighty and family-ending mess of anger. Clothes covered the floor. The bed was slashed hard and eviscerated. The wardrobe door hung from the single surviving bent screw of one hinge. A fist-size hole at head height took the blame for the lightning-streak scar beneath Cutter's watch strap.

Jenny's room was spotless. She hated things out of place. The clear desk beneath the window had two sharpened pencils at the ready in a plastic cup.

Looking out, Cutter saw a reddening of the sky. It was too early for dawn. From the direction, it could only be the Evans' house. He was heartened that somebody had seen fit to cleanse the town completely.

Through the slim vertical gap between the door and its jamb, he caught sight of his daughter's boots: red leather, white soles, white laces and a white fur trim. Her Santa boots, Debbie had called them. They had driven to the city for those boots, the last day of the half-term holiday, the weekend before she was taken. They were meant to complement the red check of the plaid skirts worn during winter term. They had argued about them. Couching it in terms he felt reasonable, he had tried to steer them towards a more sober pair of a conservative price and black leather that would take the wax and polish they already possessed, not the red ones the assistant already had in her hand.

Jenny had worn them once, on the Monday. A boy had made fun of them at school and she wouldn't wear them on the Tuesday. Her mother had tried to tell her that it was a boy's way of being friends; picking on you meant they liked you. She had blushed but hadn't budged. She returned to school in black boots. Surprised as he was, John was saddened. Once the buying was done, the red ones became her boots; they suited her and he was secretly proud of her determination. He should have told her. For the first time, he had entertained thoughts of her growing up, meeting somebody, not needing him. Maybe the boy apologised.

Jenny's cat was still waiting at the foot of her bed. It had stopped eating the evening she hadn't come home. For seven days, in which time her body was recovered, identified and buried, it circled her room, getting thinner. He had taken changes of food, milk and water, talked to the cat; a cat he had never been particularly fond of. He tried to stroke it once, to feel what his little girl had felt. It hissed at him and swiped extended claws across the back of his hand, as though he was the reason for her absence. Cutter rubbed his hand, still offended. He'd stopped taking the food that the cat had not been eating, and removed its water. Three days later it had lain down at the foot of her bed and died.

He was shocked at the condition of the remains. The skin looked as delicate as ancient parchment; the short glossy fur was gone. The spine arced between disconnected limbs. The ribs of a broken cage were piled like the jack straws of his daughter's game of pick-up. The skull was bare, the eye sockets hollow. The mouth lay slightly open, enough to let the last breath out, or possibly, at the end, realising that it needed to eat.

Vehement and irrational, Cutter had refused to move

it after it had died. Nor would he allow her mother to move it. This became the reason she left. It allowed her to leave. She refused to see the cat's devotion as a good thing.

He hadn't cried when Deborah had left. No want remained in their relationship. Their daughter hadn't been the glue that held them together, but her absence was their undoing. He had made their bedroom uninhabitable and withdrawn to the ground floor.

Looking into his little girl's room, he saw the reflection of her bed in the dressing table mirror. Her doll slept.

'I got him, darling.' His dad voice was rusty and broken-edged. 'I told you I would. It's been a while, I know.' He swallowed into his parched throat. 'Time passes.'

He leant against the wall. Tonight was right, though. The boy knew it, as well as anybody, stripped naked like he was. It was a sacrifice. He was guilty of more than surviving. It was all over his face.

'You think it got too much, the being alive?'

John Cutter looked at the glow in the sky.

'Now that he's gone, who knows, this might even become a good place to live once more. Anyway, I knew you'd like to know.'

He stood on the threshold. He stared at her desk.

'Baby – seems like it's at an end.' He took hold of the handle. Just before the door was fully closed, he stopped. 'Your mother's gone. Don't know if I told you that. If not, I'm sorry.'

The hand-made door clicked into place. The fit to frame was perfect.

Downstairs, he kept the drapes drawn across the

stairwell. He drank whisky and lay down to sleep. He couldn't. His thoughts ran like the cracks in the ceiling, tearing through sense and reason as he relived the events of the night; feeling the weight of the club, the impact of contact and hearing the boy's final breath as it squeaked out of him, compressed through the kink in his neck. He wondered where the leak would come from. The fucking priest was favourite. If not the priest, who else wouldn't be able to contain their guilt, would need to confess it, or worse, share it? Not everybody had his mental fortitude. Somebody would need to take the night's events out of the village. Of that he was certain.

John Cutter stood and dropped his trousers. He took the gouge missing from the tool rack from beneath his pillow. Sitting on his bed, he wiped his right thigh. It was partially shaven. From the groin to the knee in a parody of fish scales were dozens of crescent-shaped scars. Healed, fine and livid at the top, the lowermost were scabbed and still itchy. He positioned the gouger blade before pushing it into his thigh until the skin broke and blood seeped. He held it steady as a thin red line trickled around his leg. A single drop of blood hit the floor before he took the gouge from the wound. He used his handkerchief to wipe the blade before stemming the flow. He lay back and dozed off.

He awoke to the smell of burning. He focused on the stains and broken plaster above his head. His ears picked up revelry, jubilation, footfalls, and then quiet; quiet for a good while – until there was a knock on his door. He fastened his trousers and answered.

Deborah stood outside the house in denial of what he

91

had recently told their baby. The priest held her up. The last time he'd seen her before tonight was the last time he'd arrested her, months ago.

This wasn't the girl he had wanted; the girl whose tummy had fluttered as his fingers traced the line of her knicker elastic before sliding into the dip between her hip bone and what there was of her belly, her moaning, urging his fingers down with her hand, inviting him to explore.

She was dirtier than usual, and drunk again. She swayed and would have fallen had the priest not steadied her, his arm around her waist. She didn't look up. He wasn't sure she even knew where she was. John Cutter had never seen anyone more in need of help. He told the priest to take her away, turning and closing the door without watching them go.

He couldn't lie down again. Topping strong coffee up with whisky, he sat and listened to the rain as it swept across the village.

When he left the house, Cutter was in uniform, the priest was gone, the rain was easing and morning was on the way.

Fraser Blades, 8

*Seven years earlier*

Fraser Blades blew hard as he cleared the snow from the yard entrance. His dad, builder 'Sandy Blades – man of trades', was renowned for being late with quotes and low on estimates when compared to the final bill, but he was local. Schoolmates had told Fraser his dad was a thief.

Fraser earned a modest yet steady wage during the school holidays, cleaning tools, learning the correct proportions for mixing concrete or grout and chipping cement off old bricks and stone to be reused. Though he accepted that clearing the yard this morning was part of his remit, he hated that his fingers were blue and smarting with the cold. Through the kitchen window he saw his dad pour a healthy dram into his coffee flask and tighten the lid against the escaping steam, then take a swig from the bottle. He caught Fraser watching and pulled a mock-guilty face before making a play of offering him the whisky. Fraser frowned and shook his head in pretend chastisement, then returned to the final few yards of clearing, wishing he was in the warmth of the kitchen.

In his bedroom, Fraser kept his wages in his bank: a whisky tin with a slot punched out of the lid by a screwdriver. He had asked his dad to solder the lid on to stop him spending any of his savings. Lifting the tin to gauge the weight, he shook it close to his ear, as if wealth had a particular sound. He was an avaricious collector of money, believing it would protect him against the cold and the isolation. He didn't want to be like his dad. At the back of his unformed mind he sensed a future that would depend upon lying to his peers with a smile on his face at the service to the clink of coin in his pocket. He wanted friends, wanted to belong. His dad worked long hours alone and spent each night the same, short drinks his only companion.

Fraser thought he knew a way out. After rinsing his face, he combed his hair, wanting to look his best today for Lucy Livingstone, his future partner.

Fraser had decided to make a good show of pretending to like Lucy Livingstone. He made this decision after an opportunity presented itself on the third Saturday of September, at the harvest festival. Beneath the helium balloons and jostled by the elbows of adults, he was pretending to weigh up how many multicoloured marbles there were likely to be in the sealed glass jar. Positioning himself so that he could see beyond the jar, he observed the enthusiasm and competition of the crowd gathered around the cake stall in the corner of the class. Dismissing the short-term gain of marbles, he mingled with the adults. As he listened to the praise accorded to Lucy Livingstone's baking, Fraser watched her cakes disappear from the trestle table. He calculated how much she had raised for the school. Substituting himself for the school, he concluded she would be a good business partner, and a cake shop would be warm and happy.

On the Sunday he had taken her a speculation of chocolates and a business plan that filled one and three quarter pages of his jotter. Lucy's mother and father were both impressed with his ideas but in a way that made him think they didn't take them seriously. Fraser thought Lucy would be his ideal partner in business, as beyond the supply of cakes she wanted nothing to do with it, nervous even with the notion of marketing, sales and profit (words her parents had used in a jokey manner). But somebody had taken him seriously. At school, Heavy Bevy had snatched the pages of his proposal from Lucy's hands and studied them, refusing to give them back until he fully understood.

This morning Fraser made it his business to shelter alongside Lucy, laughing with her and the rest of the class as they watched Mr Corrigan's erratic progress towards the school, his car skating across road and track, headlights almost swallowed by the snow.

# II

Down in the hole that used to be the Evans' house, the iron bulk of the range cooker still hissed with every raindrop. It was one of the few things big enough for John Cutter to recognise as household furniture. He spat through the steam and smoke: *tsssssss*.

He drove away.

Parking at the rear of his house, Cutter left the engine running as he went to the garage. Leaving the keys in the padlock body, he hung the shackle from the hasp it usually secured. The wooden door swung easily on well-greased hinges. The lights of the car flooded the garage and cast his shadow large. The aluminium ladder hung from beam hooks down the right. Hooked down the left were three bicycles and at the far end a scooter, hula hoops, skipping ropes, roller skates, kneepads and elbow pads and a helmet. Overcome by the strength of feeling these playthings evoked, he turned away from them, accidentally knocking the canoe on the floor with his heel. It rocked as if afloat, the orange child seat in the middle bright against the green of the craft. He noticed something he'd never seen before. On the side, where Jenny would have held on, were the prints of her four fingers, made by the suncream she'd coated herself in. John Cutter closed his eyes and found the ladder by touch.

He locked the garage without seeing her fingerprints again.

The ladder safely strapped to the roof rack, he went into the house. He found the old address book. On the inside page was a number in red ink. He lifted the receiver and dialled.

'Shep? It's John Cutter.' He took a steadying breath, kept a level tone. No malice, just information. 'Your house burned down. He's dead. Thought you should know. I'll expect you.'

The receiver bounced as he dropped it in the cradle.

He drove back.

Blocking the path with his car, Cutter turned the heating up, reclined his seat and went to sleep while what was left of the Evans' house cooled down.

Waking to a cold, watery blue sky, he shivered as he walked amongst the ruins.

He stood over the buckled bedstead and the melted springs of the mattress. Amongst the springs was the suggestion of a human form. Like those from war-zone photographs of soldiers having failed to escape their burning vehicles, captured as charred remains, teeth white amongst the blackness of it all. The extremities were gone. Most of the torso and the gourd of the head remained. The contents of the cranial cavity were still slow cooking. Cutter noticed that some of the teeth were not white.

Warm between his fingers, the fused gold came loose.

He pocketed the gold and thought he knew who had started the fire.

Lucy Livingstone, 9

*Seven years earlier*

Lucy Livingstone took great care wrapping two slices of cloutie dumpling in greaseproof paper: one for each of her prospective business partners. She wanted both to try it. This morning she was entertaining the notion that baking might be her future. Her favourite moments at school were the fund-raising days of the summer and winter fairs. The treats presented by her and her mother were always the first to go and the last to be talked about. Bannocks and crumpets, shortbreads and scones, gingerbreads and dumplings, tablets and cakes, their fare as traditional and nostalgic as their way of life.

Her family was in many ways similar to the Struans, clinging to some imagined bygone age of heather and tweed. The Livingstones didn't question their place in society and knew they were not the kind of people who brought about its change. Lucy already had her mother's loose figure and, meek and expecting to inherit nothing, believed she was destined for a life of increasingly heavy body and shallow breathing, at the service of the mannie she loved.

This mannie might turn out to be Fraser, whose recent attention had flattered and scared her. His ideas were so far beyond the realms of childhood that they made her light-headed from notions of a future. What she took from his proposal was a promise of security. Her job would be to support him. She knew her place. At least she had until she had been handed a counter-proposal that Monday, this one typed and professional when compared to Fraser's pages from his jotter, neat as they were.

# 12

Deborah dreamt of barking and the skitter of frantic paws back and forth on the upper landing looking for a way out. Yelping down a staircase at the rising heat and choking fumes was reduced to a plaintive whimper for help that never came as a bedroom door was pawed. A long-abandoned whine stretched into the night as the dog spirit of the boy was purged. One final howl from high within the place the dog had called home since its body cheated death, forced out by its destruction. The smell of burning fur.

Her topcoat was on fire when she awoke. Men held her down. She kicked and tried to get free as they slapped her head, shouted, doused her with beer. She took it for another dose of abuse. Such was the power in her struggle, one only managed to hold her down by pinning her to the ground with his whole upper body weight. It finally filtered through: they were helping, telling her it was okay and that she was safe. They pointed to the burning house, fifty yards from where they'd dragged her and too far gone to save. She stopped fighting.

They lifted her up, hugged her, danced her up and down, whooped with her, shared beers and for a moment forgot what they had done to her in some recent past. She laughed and screamed and gripped tight to anybody close enough to hold, which caused them to tense, turned their smiles rigid and mouth-bound as their eyes were troubled by memories of the last time they'd held her and how little respect it had involved. Reminded of things they had no desire to recall, they left her alone. Patting her on the back, they forced a beer into her hand and went to mingle with the others of the village who had started arriving, keen to witness the end.

She overheard her name every so often but nobody came down to where she danced alone unless it was to give her another bottle, which would keep her away. It got so that everybody was between her and the burning and they were all together. Her moment was taken away. Her world was small again.

Deborah stopped her dancing when it no longer made her happy; when she was no longer happy enough to dance.

'Sabbath.' She searched for the white dress in the night. Sabbath was nowhere to be seen. 'Sabbath? Sabbath.'

She straightened her back and steadied herself, turning her head like a dazed owl, scouring the night for John Cutter. A man reached for her. She put her arms out for him. He wrapped himself around her and passed no judgement.

*Seven years earlier*

James Beverage wrapped a warm pie in a tea towel and placed it at the top of his school bag. He was the only son of the butcher, Alan Beverage, and his wife, Una. Puppy fat, gradually replaced by the combined fats of pork, beef, mutton and lamb, along with that from puddings, blood and suet, had conspired to hide his frame from view. He appeared to be constructed from circles, like a snowman, though he shone, moist and red, betraying the unchecked gluttony, the blame of which could not be pinned on him alone. The idea of pinning anything on Heavy Bevy brought to mind the singular image of bodily explosion. He hadn't seen his penis since he was seven years old and only knew he had hair growing down there because he had checked using a mirror and his sausage-fingered hands; frequently these last few weeks.

Spoiled from the day he was squeezed from between the folds of his mother's thighs, he was unused to doing without. And what Heavy Bevy didn't want to do without was Lucy Livingstone. His ire had risen the moment he'd heard of Fraser's proposal. He knew it was financially motivated and emotionally insincere. In that instant, Lucy had become the girl for him. Acknowledging that Alice Corggie was beyond him and beauty such as hers would remain so forever, Heavy also conceded that pretty girls like Jenny Cutter and Jean Ritt would only scorn him if he approached them. They would never be impressed with or see the potential in the roly-poly son of the butcher.

'No mind to all that,' his father had said when Heavy had skirted around the subject. He told his son he had 'foresight', which was much more important than looks. Thus reassured, Heavy had folded the typed business proposal in half and slid it into his jotter until delivery. He was pleased with her reaction when he handed it to her and was sure Fraser and his false intentions would be swept away by the persuasive logic of his father's argument. Heavy Bevy, like his father, was utterly convinced of the superiority of the pie over the cake. It was, like himself and Lucy, solid and substantial, not a frippery. A cake was a thing to be had after your dinner, if you still had space. A pie was your dinner. With a good pie there would often be no space. Heavy was going to get Lucy to say aye to a pie, because together they would be, as the masthead to his proposal declared, a perfect blend of savoury and sweet.

# 13

Since Mary Magnal's visit, Father Wittin had sat in the confessional all evening, behind the green velvet curtains, the overhead light turned off, wrapped in sensory deprivation. A small convector heater fought against the church's chill. He yawned as he looked at his watch. He was surprised to see it was after ten. He wasn't sure if he'd dozed off. If so, nobody had come to wake him. Nobody was coming.

He stepped out and shivered as his muscles contracted against the colder air of the nave. The cable snaked across the floor and disappeared behind the baptismal font to the nearest socket. The heater turned off and unplugged, he made his way back to the confessional, coiling the cable around hand and elbow. He left the coil on his seat. Genuflecting before the altar, he began to cross himself to pray as he raised his eyes to the stained-glass crucifixion that soared above the tabernacle. 'In the name of the ...' He stopped, his fingertips barely touching his forehead.

'God in heaven, what have they done now?'

Christ was burning. All about him panes of glass were alive with a fiery radiance that rose up the cross and lit his body, giving him more the look of Joan of Arc than the son of God, mankind's saviour.

Wittin had to bear witness.

Running down the church path, his leather soles slipped on the thickening ground frost and his arms stretched and windmilled as he bore left at the bottom before heading through the village. As he ran, he noticed the open doors of some of the houses, the escaping heat hazing up through the cones of security lights. Abandoned radios and televisions played in empty rooms. A stovetop kettle whistled. A telephone rang. A running car faced an open garage, ready to be parked up for the night. The concertina door of the fire station was pulled aside, yet the fire engine sat strangely squat and immobile on a floor that shone like quicksilver. From an open window somewhere a forgotten baby wailed. He forgot the baby himself as he took a left onto Marsh Lane and saw the house of the murdered boy entirely consumed by a roaring inferno.

The burning had drawn many more than had been at the school. The mood was celebratory, verging on delirium. He saw bottles being passed around. Whatever the parents hadn't released since they buried their children, they were releasing it now. But the other villagers: what were they here for? It dawned on him that those that hadn't been at the killing must believe the boy to be in the house and that this was a good thing.

Between them and him he recognised Deborah, outcast, staggering as though she was about to faint. He ran, clumsy and flapping in his cassock. He caught her, held her. She called him John. She nuzzled and kissed him, her mouth hot on his neck. It was only when her lips brushed the thin line of beard that she realised he wasn't John. She scratched and screamed and he had no choice but to push her away. The crowd cheered as she fell.

He was humiliated and strove to get her back up, floundering, his feet skating off the flattened grass. He realised that the cheering wasn't for them when it continued, rising in waves of intensity at each separate sound of splintering wood and snapping frame. The house was imploding. The cellar became a fire pit into which everything fell. As if by design, the exterior walls folded, one after the other, into the centre, blasting out squalls of smoke and heat that caused people to recoil or instinctively drop to the ground, protecting their heads with their arms or the hoods of their coats. When it was judged safe, arms dropped and heads lifted to look again. The villagers were awed. The flames roared into the heavens as if screaming from the very soul of the earth. Those whose impish silhouettes had moments before danced around the rim in echo of some medieval tableau, tossing in empty cans and beer bottles as the fire feasted on the boy's home, were humbled and subdued. There was no return to revelry.

As he watched them, black-backed and golden-fronted, their faces tearful, open-mouthed, childlike and guilty, Wittin wondered if, at last and at some level, they were undertaking a degree of internal examination.

Before long, the empty wooden house was gone.

Once again these people turned their backs. A line of sooty figures traipsed back to the village, wordless as soldiers returning from the Front.

The only one who remained was Deborah. She drained the single malt that was wasted on her and dropped the bottle to the floor. Wittin held her arm around his neck and put his around her, close to his side. Taking her weight, he guided her away. His hand slipped beneath her jacket. Her tummy was warm and smooth.

The guidance of Deborah aside, Wittin's return journey through the village was uneventful. Doors were closed, cars were garaged and babies slept.

Wittin knocked on John Cutter's door. When it opened, Cutter looked at Deborah but spoke to him.

'Go to hell and take her with you.'

'She's been, damn you. Look at her.'

'Then she'll know the way back.'

Cutter closed the door. Wittin looked at Deborah and sighed. He looked up to the sky.

'I fucking tried.'

Fat raindrops began to fall.

By the time he'd half dragged, half carried her to his church, they were drenched. Wittin closed the door behind them, slamming back against it as he recovered. The pair of them dripped onto the porch matting. He led her down the aisle and lowered her on to the front pew, using the armrest to support her.

Passing through the cloakroom, he turned the full heating system on for the first time that winter. Beneath his feet in the crypt the boiler grumbled to life and he could feel the vibrations up his legs. The pipes and joints that emerged from below pinged and creaked as warmth was forced through them.

When he returned from his quarters with towels, having removed his wet coat and cassock, he thought she was gone. He stopped, the towels suddenly heavy in his hands. Then he heard snoring.

She had slumped, her head falling back, her throat tight, airway occluded. After making her more comfortable, he pulled her boots off, unbuttoned her jeans and slid them off, along with her pants. Her pubic hair had the same brass sheen as his tabernacle. Her milky skin was marbled bluey-purple from the cold. He righted her, eased her arms out of her jacket and lifted her wet top, pausing to stare at her when her face was hidden and her arms held in the air. She was pallid and thin. Her stiffened nipples were raspberry pink. She shivered. He pulled the top over her head, wrapped a towel around her. He used another towel to take most of the wet from her hair as she slumped against his stomach. When she was dry, he draped the damp towel over the back of the pew.

'Right now, you come with me,' he said, lifting her to her feet. He all but carried her through the gate in the altar rails and laid her on the thick red carpet of the chancel, using one of the embroidered wedding hassocks for a pillow. He hurried to the vestry, returning with a selection of robes and vestments.

He stood above her. She looked like she'd dropped from the sky and was waiting for him. He knelt alongside her, placing the robes on the floor. He shaped his hand around her breast, lifting it up, barely squeezing, rubbing his thumb against her nipple. With the slightest pressure on the inside of her knees he was able to ease open her legs. He moved between them.

The moment his erection hit the cold of the nave, it drooped, limp and useless. He caught it before it receded back into his trousers, yanking it, slapping it, desperate to stimulate it. He seized her nipple again, tweaking it, teasing it up and letting it drop, watching it relax as if uninterested. Frantic, he touched her between the legs, amazed at how soft the hair was, rubbing with one hand, pulling with the other, forgetting she was there.

'If you're a man of God, he has low standards.'

Wittin was nailed by Deborah's gaze. He felt his cock shrink further, flaccid and pathetic. He didn't know what to do with it now he had nothing to do with it.

'Jesus.' She rolled onto her side, closing her legs, covering herself.

'Don't judge God by my actions,' he said.

'You sure they're your own?'

'Of course.'

Deborah's derisory snort sat Wittin back on his arse, the keen air rushing in through his fly.

'Father, why don't you ever blame him?'

'For what?'

'Anything.'

Wittin thought she'd finished, that her slurred words would tail off and she would leave him alone.

'You praise him for the survivors,' she said, 'but you never blame him for the disaster. It's always the same. He put the thought in your head, your cock in your hand.'

'No, he didn't.'

'Did he wake me up?'

'Maybe.'

'You glad? Or are you cursing his name?'

'You're drunk.'

'Which is why you thought you'd fuck me.'

'You're making no sense.'

He couldn't face her. He looked around his church, at the bleak corners of the transept, at the Stations of the Cross, the brass candles, the pulpit, the font, the choir stalls, the empty pews, the confessional, and the crucifix on the altar below the stained-glass Christ.

'God got me drunk,' she said, goading him. 'Maybe it was for you. You've let Him down.'

'Stop talking about Him like that.'

'Fasten yourself.'

Wittin finally let go and zipped his fly.

Deborah shivered.

'I have the heating on. It shouldn't take long.'

She looked at the pile of clothes from the vestry. Wittin grabbed them, spreading them over her nakedness. By the time he'd wrapped her in the robes, covering her feet and tucking right into the small of her back, he was thankful.

Deborah closed her eyes. Her mouth parted as she slept. He listened to each soft breath. She had freckles. He resisted the urge to lean over and touch her.

She slept soundly as Wittin placed her boots and wet clothes over the thick ribbed radiators to dry. He made sure she was comfortable then sat on the chancel steps with his back to the altar and her. Taking the cork from the holy wine, he drank from the bottle.

He was still there when Deborah stirred. He imagined she'd be trying to remember what she'd drunk, who she was with, where she was and why she was lying behind him below the altar, her head on a red velvet cushion edged with golden ropework, cocooned in his vestments. Everything would be on its side from where she lay. She would be warm. She would sniff the faint smell of incense as she stared at the sloped back of the priest who had tried to abuse her, and the row upon row of empty pews.

'Is it morning?'

'Close to.'

'Have you seen Sabbath?'

'Who?'

'My friend.'

'Can't say I have.'

'I've been abandoned.'

'You and me both.'

He tightened the slope of his back into a curl and knitted his fingers together behind his head to make himself more compact.

'What's the matter?' she said.

He unfurled.

'I don't know what I'm for any more.'

'Stop feeling sorry for yourself.'

The priest strained his neck rather than turn around to fully face her.

'I beg your pardon.'

'It wasn't meant to sound flippant,' she said, as if sensing something wasn't right. 'I'm sorry.'

'Don't mention it. I don't believe I deserve to be taken seriously.'

'You have to help yourself.'

'You're a fine one to talk.'

Wittin looked away. He took a swig from the bottle.

'Could I have some, take the edge off?'

Without turning, he offered it to her. He heard her sit up and take a mouthful.

'Ugh,' she said. 'It's sweet.'

'Fortified.'

She tapped him with the bottle and he took it from her. She lay down.

'I always liked being in church.'

'So why stop coming?'

'It stopped being a nice place.'

He couldn't help but nod at what she'd said.

'This is the cushion I knelt on,' she said, not noticing or choosing not to comment on his agreement. 'Side by side with my John, the day we exchanged vows. I was happy that day. I think everybody was. It was sunny. The church was full. There were flowers everywhere.'

'I envy you that happiness.'

'Ah, but I was happy in a different way, a floaty, dandelion-seed, out-of-body happy that made me feel so light I had to hold on to my John all the time or the gentlest of breezes could have taken me and I don't know where I would have landed, or if I would; because she was already inside me, and only I knew. We were already a family.'

'Like I said.'

'There's no point to envy, Father. Besides, it's a sin.'

'One of many.' He twisted slightly to see her. All that was visible was her head.

'Do you know, Deborah, I've never performed the sacrament of marriage. There hasn't been a wedding in this church since I was sent here.'

'Well, maybe it wasn't to be.'

'Maybe.'

She watched as he rubbed his eyes and once more regretted her flippancy.

'Does it make a priest happy, do you think, to marry somebody?'

'Depends on the somebody, I would imagine.'

'She would have been coming up to marrying age, thinking about it anyway, and university, and living in the city probably.'

'What was her name?'

'Jenny.'

'That's pretty. Short for Jennifer?'

'No,' she said.

He saw her grin pushing into the cushion.

'Long for Jen. Jen Cutter.'

Wittin had a smile on his face as he shifted his body around.

'Sure it's nice that the memory of her can still make you happy.'

'Mm, you're right.'

Her eyes were partially closed. She drifted away.

They had spoken of dead children; what else? But without what he was so used to seeing and hearing from his potential parishioners. Memories of Jenny had taken her to a good place. He knew it wasn't always the case, but it was possible. She looked happy in her sleep and he assumed she was thinking about Jenny still. He sat watching her, the sweetness of her face on the wedding cushion. She was a pleasure to be with. When she came back, a wee while later, he had to look away.

'How are you feeling?' he said.

'Shitty, as usual.'

Wittin offered her the almost empty bottle as she sat up. She shook her head. He drained it.

'Warm enough?'

'Mm. Warmest I've been since summer.' She realised she was naked. He watched her hands move beneath the robes. 'Where are my clothes?'

'They're drying,' he said.

She looked to where he pointed.

'You undressed me?'

'You were soaked to the skin. I couldn't let you sleep in wet clothes. You'd catch your death.'

'What did you do?'

'Sure, I—'

'What did you fucking do? Did you touch me?'

'What? I mean, you don't remember what happened?'

'Do you think I could live with myself if I remembered? I try not to. I don't know why I ever let them do it.'

He tensed. She saw it, the move to the defensive. He felt condemned.

'Something happened.'

'I undressed you, is all.'

'Enjoy it?'

'I was just doing what needed to be done. You know how it is, you get caught up in the time of things, not really space to be doing any enjoying.'

'You don't even believe yourself. You sound nervous.' Deborah felt between her legs. 'You didn't fuck me? Really?'

Wittin put his hands up to stop her, uncomfortable at the directness of her question, unused to talk of a sexual nature. He saw the robes slipping as she sat up, revealing bare shoulders for a second before she covered herself.

'We didn't,' he said.

'We?'

'I couldn't.'

'You tried?'

'I wanted to, I'm sorry.'

'So you did try and fuck me?'

'Not really. I wanted to know what it was like, how it felt, anything. I didn't want to hurt you.'

'You didn't think I'd mind?'

'I thought you looked beautiful.'

'You're a fucking priest.'

His hands were trembling as he ran them through his hair, joining them together, once more encaging his head as though its contents were too much to bear.

'I was sure you wouldn't know. You were so drunk, away with it, unconscious really.'

'Oh Lord,' said Deborah. Her dry, humourless croak hung in the arid silence of the church. 'I should have been safe.'

'Nothing happened. You woke up. You saw me.'

'About to fuck me?'

'I'm glad you woke up,' he said. 'That it didn't happen.'

'Good for you. I'm glad you're glad. You still sinned.'

'I know. And I'm sorry. It was against everything I claim to believe in.'

'It was against me. Fuck! And I thought I was going to hell.'

'I'm sorry.'

'Father, I thought you were nice.'

'But nothing happened.'

'That doesn't make it right.'

'It makes it better, surely?'

'Not to me.'

Wittin stood, unsure for a moment whether his legs would support him.

'Running away?'

'More wine.'

When he returned from the sacristy with another bottle, she was no longer naked. She was by the altar, dressed in his alb, aglow with the stained morning light of the east window, and all he could think of was angels.

'You're not going to hell,' he said.

She turned as he approached. Standing in front of the tabernacle, she had the look of an icon, presented to him for him alone to see. He bowed his head and made the sign of the cross before stepping up to her.

She took the wine off him. 'Not today, anyway.'

'Not ever.'

He trembled as he held her arm.

'It's a bit late to be saving me, don't you think?'

He withdrew his hand.

'Will you be saying anything?' he asked. Ashamed as he was, he didn't look away.

'Will you?'

'Sure, why would I be mention ...' His words petered out as he realised what Deborah was asking.

'I would say the two things hardly compare.'

'Of course you would. You're a man.'

'I'm a priest.'

'You're supposed to be,' said Deborah, with an edge to her voice that muted Wittin. 'You still can be. We're both asking for each other's silence. I want it for all our sakes.'

'Shame on you, Deborah.'

'Me?'

Wittin turned from her, walked the length of the nave and slipped the lock. Looking back from the porch, he saw Deborah standing in the sanctuary he had just left.

Lucy Magnal, 8

*Seven years earlier*

Lucy Magnal scanned the street. She was wary of stepping out of the church behind the handful of other morning parishioners.

'Lucy, will you stop being silly.'

'I'm not going to school.'

'Oh yes you are,' said Mary. 'It is my duty to send you – and you, young lady, have an even greater responsibility to use the brain that God gave you. Think about the poor black babies in Africa. They don't even get the chance.'

Lucy was the baby of the class, fatherless and blindly religious. Fed bible for breakfast and scripture for supper, attending morning Mass with Mary, her mother, each day before school.

'They laugh at me.'

Mary Magnal took a wooden crucifix from the side pocket of her handbag. She placed it in Lucy's hand and wrapped her fingers around it.

'God's friendship is the only one you need. You've been told what to do about the others: pity them.'

The Todds had been the first to laugh and point at Lucy, their eyes almost popping out at the recognition, hooting that she attended church so often she was starting to look like the priest, Father Finnegan. It was said without spite, but the rest of the class took up the cause, and within the space of one day she was being referred to as Lucy Finnegan. Her mother had complained. The teacher and the parents of the PTA had ignored her remonstrations.

Her father had been unable to intervene.

Mary Magnal went quiet on the matter.

Lucy's behavioural problems thus began when she realised she was voiceless, save for the reedy whine she managed to produce that only invited more laughter and ridicule when used in anger. There was no one to stand up for her. She didn't cry. She took to distant benches and solitary walks around the school boundary, chewing her way through a packed lunch of sliced-bread monotony that offered little solace or nourishment. When that was finished, she found a vantage point and observed her peers from behind her thicket-like fringe, looking for weakness.

Her comments, when they came, were sly, vindictive and careless, rooted as they were in her own elevated separation and growing disregard for others. They also betrayed the influence of a higher hand, and the teacher suspected she had been coached in what to say by Father Finnegan in compensation for his inability to intervene publicly, thereby consolidating his ungodly transgressions.

Most of Lucy's vitriol was saved for Alice Corggie, because her popularity was effortless and she bore it as though deserved. Slut, whore, narcissus, jezebel: all words that Lucy internalised rather than sling across the classroom or playground. Any expression against Alice would be foolhardy.

'I'll pity Alice today,' said Lucy.

'You do that. You pity her hard.'

Mary pushed Lucy into the morning and closed the door behind them as if they were leaving home.

# 14

The message was short. The handset was still cold in Shep's hands when the buzz of the dialling tone filled his ear and the news screamed inside his head.

'Who was it?' Rebecca said.

'John Cutter.'

She tensed. 'Has he done something?'

'There was a fire,' said Shep. 'He's dead.'

He saw straight away that she was relieved, and it troubled him. She never mentioned their son.

She put her red duffle back on. Sprightly fingers skipped from toggle to toggle, ready in seconds. In the moments since the news, her skin appeared to have firmed and she looked younger.

'I'm going to church,' she said.

'You're just back. Why do you need to go again?'

'To pray, Shep. To pray.'

'To give thanks?'

'Shame on you, Shep Evans, I will not have you judge me, or speculate on the subject of my prayers for that matter.'

'Okay, okay,' he said, his hands up and open.

She gathered her hair into a ponytail and secured it with a red cherry bobble. He noticed that her hands now shook.

'You could walk with me,' she said, not raising her gaze to his.

Without answering, Shep kissed her where the hair was pulled tight and smooth and the black shone with the blue-green of a magpie's wing. He put his arms around her and hugged her for a moment. She didn't relax or hug him back; she was already easing away, down the hallway.

'Rebecca?' She turned, pale blue eyes over her raised collar. 'Do you say his name? In church, I mean?'

'What I say in church is between me and God. You know that, Shep.'

'I know. I'm sorry.'

He watched her walk down their path to the pavement. She crossed the road and entered the avenue of trees that lined the driveway to the church opposite their house; the reason they lived in this house.

'What's left to pray for, Rebecca?'

After a few steps her head dipped and she hurried to the church door. It looked as though she could be crying. Shep hoped she was.

Even with the windows open, the conservatory soon filled with cigar smoke. The ceiling fan moved it around. Shep sat back as he watched a blackbird dancing on the lawn, imitating light rain, cocking its head to listen for movement before stabbing the ground with its yellow beak. It pulled a worm from the lawn and swallowed it whole. Two blue tits pecked at the nuts hanging from the porch of the summer house at the end of the garden. A redwing pulled berries from the holly bush, which was laden, the portent of a harsh winter ahead. He cursed the neighbour's cat as it leapt from the hedgerow. Even though it missed the blackbird, it cleared the garden of all birds. He drew on the cigar, expelling the smoke as he picked up the phone and dialled.

'Donald, hello, it's Shep. How's things with you?'

He took a long breath and let it out gradually as he listened. 'Actually, no, things are not fine, that's why I'm calling. I need to take a few days' holiday ... No, no, it's not Rebecca. There's been a death in the family ... Thank you, that's much appreciated ... Yes, it was someone close – my son, sorry, our son ... We didn't really see each other. You know what families can be like ... Thank you again, I'll pass them on to Rebecca. Okay, I'll see you next week then. Bye, Donald.'

When Rebecca came back from church, he was still sitting in the cane lounger, finishing his cigar. The blackbird was back on the lawn.

'So, praying help?'

She looked confused and disappointed as she stared at him, her coat still toggled up.

'Shep, you've been smoking in the house.'

'Still am, but only here, in the conservatory.'

'But the rules. Why didn't you go outside?'

'I didn't want to.'

She was wary and unsure as she studied him. Her fingers twisted within themselves like snakes.

'Anyway,' he said, 'they're your rules.'

'But Shep—'

'I'm going back.'

'But you agreed. Besides, if it was a fire ...'

'There'll be remains, something to identify. There has to be a burial.'

The lounger creaked as he leant forward to put his cigar stub in the ashtray.

'Rebecca, I need to apologise.'

'But—'

'To him. That's where I'll find my peace; if there's any to be had.'

She was shaking her head, and the eyes that implored him not to go were already flooding.

'Come here.'

He took her in his arms, tried to calm the quivering, stall the hyperventilating. Lowering his voice to console her, his words were almost a croon. He couldn't disguise the dread that weighed each word down.

'Believe me, Becca, I'm not thrilled at the prospect of returning to the village. You could stay here.'

Her arms tightened around him.

Wittin didn't know where else to go. He walked through the village knowing he wasn't required. Last night had been the end. He hadn't stopped them. They had confirmed the death of their belief. What he had tried to do to Deborah felt like the death of his. It was easy to imagine his church in flames. When he got to the Evans' house, John Cutter was there, in uniform, dropping things into evidence bags.

'Find anything?' said Wittin, half expecting to be ignored, not really wanting an answer.

Looking up, Cutter motioned him to the aluminium ladder that was lashed to the sole remaining stanchion, the only access into the pit.

The ground retained the heat of the fire. Wittin

squelched through warm puddles of rainwater, and his shoes and trouser hems were soiled with ash slurry by the time he'd negotiated his way to Cutter.

Cutter didn't ask where Deborah was.

Wittin didn't tell him.

Cutter had one of his hands behind his back. He wore a cracked sneer, which held menace in the light of last night's events.

'Guess who?'

He thrust a skull into Wittin's face. His manner was playful, but he lost most of the sneer. Wittin pulled away. The skull had survived the fire but was cracked and black. A metal cross had fused to it, melting into the nose and eye socket. Cutter polished the surface of the cross with his sleeve, a grim Aladdin, quickly revealing a silver shine.

'Finnegan,' he said. 'Your predecessor.'

Wittin stared at the skull. 'What do you want me to say?'

'Alas, poor Padraig?' Cutter said. 'It's nice that you finally meet, don't you think?'

Cutter's gaze was glassy and unreadable, his face set. He flipped the skull into the air and caught it, his fingers through the eye sockets as though he was preparing to bowl. He moved aside as Wittin made to leave, revealing the charred remnants on the bedsprings. Wittin looked elsewhere and fought the urge to vomit. Drawn to look again, he tried to focus on Finnegan's skull, which was preferable, searching the cross for the Celtic pattern, dents, sooty shadows in the image of Christ, anything but the thing on the bed.

'Who is it?'

'I'll be telling them it's their boy,' said Cutter.

'What?'

'I called his parents. They're on their way.'

'You knew where they were?'

'Always have. This day's been coming. I owed them the courtesy.'

'Why?'

'They're next of kin. Besides, we used to be close.'

It was Cutter's casual tone that upset Wittin more than his intentions.

'John, don't you see how wrong this is?'

Cutter grinned. 'And last night was right?'

Wittin felt the ground burning the soles of his feet.

'What did she ever see in a man like you?' he said.

Cutter's expression clouded.

'Well at least that knocked the smile off your face.'

Wittin held his place as Cutter closed the gap between them and put his face right up close.

'Don't you presume to judge me, or so help me God I will make you regret it.'

'How could I not? I saw you kill that boy. I witnessed you discarding your wife when she needed help.'

'Yes, I did kill that boy. Everybody who was in that glade knows, and they all helped; he helped.' Cutter gestured to the remains on the bed. 'And they were glad.'

'I know, dead children.'

Cutter bristled and left no distance at all between himself and Wittin.

'Understand this. One priest disappeared and no questions were asked. It could happen again, believe you me.' Wittin creased as Cutter punched Finnegan's skull into his stomach. 'She left me.'

He was still folded around the skull that he held to himself like a rugby ball as he watched Cutter spread a clean tarpaulin over the substitute remains.

'You didn't say who it was.'

'We're going to need another postman.'

Wittin cursed as he watched the tarpaulin tighten and heard the zip of cable ties as Cutter worked around the bed.

Eleanor 'Muchis' Souter, 6

*Seven years earlier*

Ed Munson heard the clump of her wellingtons first. Three or four steps into the shop, they stopped. She was at the end of the sweet counter, her attention flitting from chocolate to candy to bon-bon to marshmallow as she worked her way along. She liked the liquorice twirls with the aniseed jelly in the centre but her granny wouldn't allow her to have those before school because they made her teeth black. Muchis thought this was unreasonable but was happy to forget that she was the only child allowed to have sweets before school at all; one of her granny's many indulgences.

'Muchis that, Mr Munson?'

He told her. She pursed her mouth and creased her nose in consideration before pointing to another item.

'Muchis that, Mr Munson?'

He told her.

Some mornings she could go through practically all he had to offer. But this morning she quickly settled upon a red box of chocolates tied with a golden ribbon on a high shelf above the rows of sweetie jars.

'Muchis that, Mr Munson?'

'How much was it yesterday?'

'I can't remember.'

'Did you have enough?'

'No.'

'And have you got the same amount of money today?'

'I think so. A wee bit more maybe.'

'Well I'd say you haven't got enough again. Anyway, that's way too big a box of chocolates for a wee lassie like you.'

To Munson's surprise, Muchis spun away from the confectionery and crossed the shop. She pointed at a gift set of soaps and creams he had ordered in for the coming Christmas. He'd been thinking along the lines of a last-minute present or stocking filler.

'Muchis that, Mr Munson?'

'Well, that's expensive.'

'More than the chocolates?'

'No.'

'Have I got enough?'

She was hopeful as she approached the newspaper counter. She opened her clammy hand for Ed Munson to count the warm coins.

'No,' he said. 'I'm afraid not, darling. But tell me, what are you wanting with a box of smellies like that? I thought sweeties were your thing.'

'For my granny. It's her birthday.'

'When?'

'I'm not sure, soon though. My daddy sent a letter. He said I should be thinking about what I want to buy her.'

'Oh, I see. And you want to help her stay all glamorous?'

Her face lit up at this suggestion and she nodded so hard her hat slipped and her face disappeared behind her shifting curls. Munson waited as she swept them aside to look at him.

'You really want the smellies?'

'Yes please.'

'Okay. Do you want to save?'

'Where?'

'Here.'

Muchis frowned. 'How?'

Ed Munson took his pad from beside the till and turned to a fresh page. He put the price of the gift box at the top of the page. Alongside, he printed her name: ELEANOR SOUTER.

'See this big number?' he said.

'Uh huh.'

'That's how much the smellies cost. Show me your money again.'

He took five silver coins from her.

'That's fifty, okay?'

'Okay.'

'So if we take fifty from the big number, that new number is how much you still need to pay. We can do it a little bit at a time.'

'But what if—'

'Don't worry.'

Ed Munson came from behind the counter, retrieved the smellies and put them behind him, above the cigarettes and tobacco.

'That's yours. I won't sell it to anybody else, I promise.'

She stared at it as if she'd won a prize.

'Thank you, Mr Munson.'

'Don't mention it. And you still have enough for a wee mix-bag. You want to pick?'

She ran to the big tray of sweets starting at a penny.

'Muchis that, Mr Munson?'

Ed Munson laughed to himself and enjoyed filling her little paper bag. When she had finished and paid him, she fixed him with an inquisitive stare.

'Should I tell my granny that you think she's glamorous?'

'Aye,' he said, 'if you like.'

'Okay. You want a cola chew?'

'No, I won't, thank you. You enjoy them.'

'I will. Bye, Mr Munson.'

'Bye.'

She put a chew in her mouth. Her wellingtons dragged across the tiles. She straightened her hat as she walked out of the door into the still-falling snow.

# 15

Deborah inspected herself in the mirror and was surprised she had the cheek to grin. She was Friday-night clean in Sunday-morning clothes. Her skin shone and her hair was brushed tight into a precious-metal ponytail that bounced from side to side as she walked through the village.

The overhead bell rang and heads turned as she pushed through Munson's door and walked the length of the sweet counter looking for the fruit-flavoured chews that had been Jenny's Friday treat. Something about her made Ed Munson wave payment away when she took out her purse.

'Thanks, Mr Munson.'

'No bother, Debbie. Good to see your old self back in the shop.'

'You think my old self still suits me?'

'Aye. It always did.'

'Maybe I'll try it again for a wee while.'

'Aye, you do that, see how it goes.'

Deborah's attention was caught by the box of smellies, dust free and gleaming above the cigarette display.

'It's a shame she never took them.'

'It is. She couldn't, they weren't paid for.'

'I thought …'

'By Muchis.'

'That's nice,' she said. 'I like that you still call her that.'

'Eleanor doesn't feel right, not to me.'

'People still pay?'

'Times over, every month.'

'It's strange, what we do.'

'To keep them here?'

'Yes.'

'The money. It goes into the "smelly" box.' Ed Munson indicated a plastic sweet box with a slot cut into its lid, a quarter full with notes and coins. 'It helps fund a bursary, for a writer. Keeps Kerr here for me.'

Deborah lifted her chews from the counter.

'Some good did come.'

'Not enough.'

'No, never enough.'

They were both relieved to hear the door chime as another customer entered.

'Thanks again,' she said, holding the chews up as she gave Ed Munson a small wave.

She could hear them already as the door closed behind her and she stepped back onto the pavement, the customers and assistants rushing to Ed Munson and asking about every word they'd already heard. 'Well now, what do you think of that? ... Almost back to her old self ... Some change, right enough ... Maybe John will take her back now, do you think?'

All it had taken was for that boy to be dead.

Cutting across Main Street and alongside the hotel took her out of their sight. Wrapping her coat around her against the shadow cold, she soon worked her way down to Marsh Lane, passing the length of the long side-walls of village homes, avoiding being seen. The brittle vegetation crisped underfoot as she crossed the corner of the marsh to the break in the fence that led into the school grounds.

Walking anticlockwise through the small circle of trees, keeping as much distance as she could from the fresh grave, Deborah made her way from six to twelve o'clock, towards the furthest tree: Jenny's. It was the tallest, spindliest tree, but Deborah also thought it was the prettiest. It stood slightly apart, as if late to join or eager to leave. An uncertain tree was how she considered it. An almost belonging, half smiling, bending in its boots and wholly necessary kind of tree. It even had its own smell, a freshness that the others had lost as moss and other growths had colonised the damp and light-deprived trunks of her classmates.

Sabbath was already sitting at the base of the tree when Deborah arrived. The girl looked up.

'How did you know this was the right tree?' Deborah asked.

'You must have told me,' said Sabbath.

'I suppose.'

'Aren't you happy to see me?'

'Surprised, after last night. Today feels different. I do.'

'I know what you mean. It's okay, though, it's not like you're late. I just thought you'd come here at some point.'

Deborah sat next to her.

'Jenny was late leaving the house on the day it happened.'

'How so?'

'She had a hissy-fit, completely out of character, about

her brand-new boots.' She smiled at the recollection. 'Little-girl boots; red with white soles and laces and white fur around the top.'

'They sound nice.'

'They were. She didn't want to wear them. John was having none of it. "You're going to school in your new boots, young lady," he said, "or you're not going at all. It's up to you." They were the last words he said to her as he left for work.'

'That's sad,' said Sabbath.

'It's a shame, because he loved her so much, and he told her often.'

'He should have told her that morning.'

'I know. But there was something about Jenny that day, a defiance we hadn't seen before. She wouldn't tell us who'd picked on her. John couldn't cope with it, so he left. I liked it, so I gave in. She sat on the stairs for ten minutes and I was thinking about valuable school time ticking away, so I let her change back into her old black and too-tight boots, reasoning with her that the red ones would take a while to get used to, that sometimes a thing in the shops looks just the ticket, but when you get it home it suddenly looks too big or bright to belong in your life. It was just a matter of giving them time, breaking them in. I wish I'd stood my ground, like John did.'

Sabbath put her hand over Deborah's.

'It wasn't your fault.'

'He made me pay as though it was; still is.'

'Don't let him. Got any coins?'

'Know what? I do,' said Deborah, pulling loose change from her purse and showing it to Sabbath. 'Ed Munson wouldn't let me pay for Jenny's sweets. The way he looked at me made me feel pretty again.'

'You are pretty,' said Sabbath in a matter-of-fact kind of way.

'Thank you.'

'So make a wish then.'

Deborah looked through the trees at the boy's grave.

'I don't know what to wish for any more.'

'There must be something, but don't tell me, or it won't come true.'

'Okay.'

When she got up, Deborah was faced with her past wishes. Each was a coin pushed into the cracks in the bark of the Jenny-tree; coins that Deborah now rubbed with her fingers, counting the years, weighing the regret, until a chill passed through her body like a charge. The protruding edges were shiny and polished, sly winks from someone else. Someone else who might be behind her, watching her hand poised over the coins, unsure as to whether she should run or stay.

Sabbath was gone.

'Hello?'

Nothing.

'I'm not leaving,' she said, surprised at the strength in her voice and how quickly she had made up her mind. 'You should come out. I'd like to meet you, know what you thought about when you were here.'

It was absolutely still. The harder she searched, the more her eyes de-focused and her vision swam, forcing her to blink. There was no one there apart from her. She sighed as sunlight broke through and a breeze blew the sinister out of the trees, along with skeletal leaves, down feathers, dried grass and the glint of a tumbling sweet wrapper that caught in the frayed hem of her jeans. The moment she saw it Deborah knew who had stood here and run his fingers over her wishes. The wrapper was folded into a perfect silver sailing boat.

Breathless, she gripped the Jenny-tree for support.

Deborah sat at the base of the tree, her back against the trunk as she chewed her way through the fruit sweets that had been Jenny's favourites. Jenny wouldn't eat them. Looking at the nine silver boats she held in her hand, she knew that now, nobody would. He had left them in the shelter of a trough between two roots of the Jenny-tree. How long ago, she could only guess. Maybe he'd sat where she sat, enjoying the same citrus tang that made her salivate. Now that the feeling of invasion had passed, she was curious as to what he would have thought. She had no exclusive claim on this tree, this patch of land, or the feelings evoked by it. Deborah felt calmer. She was letting go.

In the classroom glade, the grave was obvious. The mound was smooth and the grass slippery and bruised. The spade looked like an invitation to dig him back up again, so she cast it aside. She used the boats to make a small cross on the mound, five down – four across. She crossed herself, though did not pray, as if that would be going too far, too quickly.

Kerr Munson, 7

*Seven years earlier*

Kerr Munson had spent the previous evening writing all about Dog Evans and Jonny Raffique; documenting the events, and the effect Jonny had had on the class on Dog's first day back at school after suspension.

Kerr Munson was the happiest boy in the class. He couldn't speak but that didn't stop the rest of the class asking him questions. Calvin Struan had called him the Dummy, once. The word, exported from Struan House, had earned him a severe communal beating. He was saved by Kerr's wordless intervention.

Kerr's world delighted him. His articulation, when needed, was rendered through an ever-changing repertoire of hand signals, too erratic and nebulous to ever be corralled into an alphabet. Emotions were the hardest thing to get a grip on, running through his hands like water in a sieve. Occasionally frustration would force out tears and a rhythmic punching of his left hand with his right, as if the left was refusing to talk, to get the point across. A sudden separation of his hands as his fingers rampaged through his hair, looking for the key to fit the lock that would open and allow him to communicate. His hands always came away empty. He would grin, slap a palm against the dome of his forehead as though it was his own fault and try again as he finger-combed his hair back into some kind of order.

The irony of his situation was that Kerr Munson had a dazzling vocabulary and exercised comprehensive control over it. The limited palette of formal sign language frustrated him and was too slow. His own rapid and idiosyncratic delivery was beyond the grasp of his peers. Kerr Munson's internal happiness, the contentment that so gnawed at Dog Evans, came from the fullness of expression he achieved with the written word. His diary was dense with detail and description. His observations, mature beyond his years, were a running log of his life, open all the time, alongside his schoolwork, his breakfast, his dinner, and with him in his bed; all unread in his lifetime.

That Tuesday morning, arriving at school later than he usually did due to snow, Kerr Munson scanned the playground and took the time to quickly jot down that there was no sign of Dog Evans, Jonny was standing with the elder boys, though Calvin Struan was slightly on his own, Mr Corrigan hadn't arrived yet, the snow on the roof was at least two feet deep, it was still dark, and then he noticed the broken ground of the bird's grave.

# 16

Wittin's church was warm but empty. His nose and ears tingled with the change of temperature and the ongoing buzz from the alcohol. Finnegan's skull swung in his left hand, held by the eye sockets as John Cutter had done. He hid it in the confessional.

The vestments were piled where Deborah had slept. He picked them up and folded them neatly. Lifting the last, the one that had been closest to her, he believed he saw the vague outline of her body, still pressed into the thick pile of the carpet. He defined the line of her back between hips and shoulder blades, her ankles less so as her shape grew indistinct. He connected indentations and scuffs to create a picture of her lying there in much the same way the farmers, poets and astronomers had formed constellations of stars into giants, animals and objects; desiring order and significance. He knelt, went to cross himself, but stopped. On hands and knees, his head to the ground, he assumed the position of the penitent. Instead of praying, he sniffed. It was Deborah. She filled him. He was drunk again. He wondered if she still hoped for another baby. He told himself she was wrong; it wasn't too late for him to save her. They could both start again. It struck him as the least that should happen. He would take her away.

A short while later, Wittin had opened another bottle and sorted and boxed the possessions he would carry with him. His dog collar lay on the chest of drawers.

Connor Gardner, 5

*Seven years earlier*

Connor Gardner was sheltering on the bench beneath the slide with Robbie and Cameron Voar. They called it the wigwam. The older kids didn't go there. Connor was yawning when he spied Jean and Jenny as they came through the gate.

'Quick, quick.' He tried to hide, but Robbie and Cameron were already betraying him, shouting and pointing.

'He's here, he's here.'

The girls made a beeline for them.

'Well, what about you two, you're not very good friends at all, are you?' said Jean, leaning into the wigwam to tickle Robbie and Cameron, which was what they wanted. 'I think we'd have spotted him anyway, don't you, Jenny?'

'Even behind you two,' said Jenny.

Connor sat back, grinning and not sure where to look under the scrutiny of the two older girls. Jenny grabbed the peak of his bunnet and he quickly clamped both hands on his head to stop her pulling it off.

Connor's hair was a firework of ginger spirals that outshone a kind and warm face of freckles and hazel eyes. He had a pathological fear of the barber and point-blank

refused to go. His mother didn't force him. The screaming hysterics of the last visit had reduced her to mush.
His bald father was philosophical. 'Enjoy it while you
have it,' he said, seeing no great need to donate his son's
crowning glory to the barber-shop floor.

It grew.

It didn't get long; it got big, then bigger. Until his
mother decided enough was enough and invested in a
tub of Brylcreem.

Each morning thereafter he would arrive for class
with his head like a polished helmet, greased down tight
against his skull 'so you can concentrate'. As the day
unwound, so did his hair. Connor had taken to wearing
his hat at all times, even during gym. Jenny let go.

'Wee Connor,' said Jean, arms akimbo, an exaggerated
frown on her face, 'why were you trying to hide from us?'

Connor couldn't help but smile as he tried to make
himself smaller, his head sinking down as he tucked his
chin into his chest, his arms tight by his sides.

'There must be a reason.' Jenny bent to the level of the
boys, looked from one to another and then settled her
gaze on Connor. 'Why else would he hide?'

'I wonder what it could be?'

'His button,' said Jenny as her slender index finger
worked its way under Connor's chin. He wriggled and
writhed on the spot, eventually twisting his neck and
revealing the undone top button of his shirt. The girls
cooed with delight and Connor knew the pretence was
over. They sat him upright and set to work.

'Not buttoned up properly again. What are you like?'
said Jenny.

'At least you've got your shoes on the right feet today,' said Jean, as between them they fastened his buttons and straightened his tie. One final check and Connor was lifted from his seat and put into their bag.

'Bye, Connor,' said the twins in unison, used to seeing Connor carted off most mornings. Jack Todd heard them and took his chance to jump into Connor's place amongst the boys for a heat.

Being the smallest boy in the school, Connor had been adopted by those girls with a nascent maternal streak as their living doll, practice baby and obligation. His size and weight meant they could sit him in a holdall and carry him around the playground, a handle each, taking turns. Jean and Jenny made their way across to Maggie and Ronah, two of Connor's other mothers. Connor was slung so low and the snow lay so thick that he left a trail between their footprints. He could feel it through the bag, rushing below him. He sat back and imagined he was on a sledge.

Jean and Jenny looked down at him in expectation, waiting for him to try and escape. Attempting to get out was his part of the game. Each time he did, they would gang up on him and tickle him hard enough to make him weak and remind him who was in charge, at least until their game was over.

This morning he was tired. Out of bed too late to enjoy his breakfast, he still wanted the cuddle he usually got from his mum, who was also running late. As they were passing Maggie and Ronah, Connor made one feeble attempt to get out of the bag, pretending to struggle so as to force the girls to touch him and mould him back into their makeshift cradle. He enjoyed giving in to them, being told he was adorable as they tweaked his apple cheeks. He lay back, surrendering to the rock and sway of carriage. With the four watching over him and snow melting as it hit his face, Connor Gardner dozed off. The proxy mothers were delighted, their maternal abilities confirmed at such an early age. They were naturals; they would be good mums.

He remained good-natured as they fussed over him ten minutes later, the youngest in the school, waking in their care, surrounded by the girls of the class except Lucy Magnal, who all agreed he looked like a baby Jesus. He rubbed his eyes. His glowing face gave the impression that it had been structured by happiness; his soft bones shaped by a strong smile of clustered pearls, baby teeth displaced by the second growth but not yet ready to leave. He flushed at the attention of the girls and it was to his chagrin that he needed looking after at all.

When he stepped out of the bag he was determined to be grown up for the rest of the day and made yet another mental note for the following morning to check his buttons, his zip, his bag and his tie. He knew that every morning they would inspect him upon arrival and find the one thing that had slipped his mind or he had forgotten to do; the one thing that meant he needed to be mothered. Not any more, he thought to himself. He yawned and went to stand with the older boys, who looked as if they were sharing a secret. They were talking about growing up. Connor thought he should listen.

# 17

When John Cutter returned to his home in the evening, he found Lynne Storrie waiting for him. She was upset. Her mascara no longer did her any favours. She ran to his car before he had time to get out.

'Something's wrong, John, something bad's happened to Nugget, I just know it, and I think I know what and I can't bring myself to say the words because they're too awful. I just don't think I can say them.'

He could see the lump of Nugget's nugget in his pocket. Even as she spoke, he was speculating on its value.

'Lynne, slow down. I can't make any sense of what you're saying. Get in. I'll drive you home. You can tell me all about it in the car.'

'Why can't we talk here, John?'

'It's my home. This sounds like it might be work. Get in.'

Lynne walked around and got in the passenger side. She slammed the door.

'Warm enough?' She nodded. 'Something's wrong, you say?'

'Very.'

'Okay,' he said as he reversed back onto the road. 'Take your time, nice and clear now. Tell me why.'

She held onto the words for a while, eyes closed, swaying slightly, thinking how to start.

'Nugget went to the house.'

'The house?'

'Dog's house, last night, just after what happened.'

'Why? That makes no sense.'

'The money.'

'Money?'

'I tried to stop him, John, but he was having none of it. He had this notion about getting there first, not being beaten to it by somebody who didn't deserve it. It was like paranoia or something, as though he had some divine right to it.'

'Lynne.'

'He wouldn't listen to me.'

'Lynne.' He braked hard to snap her out of it. The car skidded before stopping and she braced herself against the dashboard, expecting a collision.

'I'm sorry,' he said. 'I didn't mean to ... What money?'

A single line creased her brow as John Cutter examined her, waiting.

'The money that was sent,' she said. 'That Nugget's been posting through the boy's door for years. You didn't know?'

'Rumours.' Cutter turned his attention back to the road and continued the drive towards the Storrie house. 'How much?

'Enough. More than, maybe. He didn't know exactly.'

'Enough to leave?'

'To stop being poor was all he wanted.'

'But could he have left? Gone, with all the money?'

'No,' she said. 'He wouldn't leave me and Bru.'

'Did Bru come home?'

147

'No.'

'So he's still with Nugget somewhere?'

Lynne nodded. John Cutter thought about the loss of a good dog as he drove in silence to the front door of Nugget and Lynne's house. He moved the gear into neutral and pulled the handbrake. He turned the key and the engine died. They sat for a moment. The windscreen began to mist.

'Lynne, do you think killing the boy was a good thing?'

'Now, I'm not sure it matters.'

'How so?'

'Nobody will miss him.' She smeared make-up across her face as she wiped, the scarlet nail varnish flashing. 'Not like I'd miss Nugget.'

'Well, it appears somebody will.'

She looked at him, her bovine eyes magnified by the swell of tears.

'Shep and Rebecca are coming back.'

'But how …'

'Somebody called them; knew where they were, somehow.'

'Who? Why?'

He offered the palms of his hands in ignorance.

'Anyway, there was a body, after the fire. From what you're telling me, it looks like it must be Nugget's. I'm sorry, I really am.'

He watched the waterworks, thick and quick, slicking down her chin and neck, into her cleavage.

'Thing is, Lynne, we're going to need a body, something to show them, to bury. You understand, don't you?'

Lynne shook her head against the whole idea as Cutter

continued talking. 'I'm thinking we give them Nugget's remains, from the fire. They can take them away with them if they like, bury him elsewhere, get some closure for themselves, get on with their own lives without asking any more questions – allow us to get on with ours. Isn't that what you want?'

'But Nugget?'

'We'll honour him, in church if needs be. Somehow we'll acknowledge his passing and the sacrifice he made, you made, for us.'

'But he didn't. He was killed in the fire. Who started it? John, do you know who started it?'

'I ... well, I was thinking it was probably Nugget. He was the only one there.'

'No.'

'Lynne, I'm not comfortable casting aspersions, particularly about the dead, but you know what he was like. He was stimulant-inclined, shall we say? Was he drunk when he left here, high? Was he smoking again?'

'I gave him whisky, and pills. They were supposed to be for courage.'

Cutter paused. 'He didn't really want to go?'

Lynne turned away. Her crying worsened. She sat with both hands covering her face, muffling the wail. He pulled her close as if to comfort her. She was already finding a way to blame herself. He didn't understand it. It was a great day. This whole fucking village was crying.

'Anything else you want to share with me, Lynne?'

She got out of the car without saying another word and approached the side door of what she had just been told was her house. She stood on the step and hesitated. She cleaned her face with both hands.

'Nug?'

Cutter left her waiting for an answer as he backed out on to the road.

As Cutter drove through the village, John Longfield, farmer and retained firefighter, ran down the apron of the station house in his overalls, waving his hands for him to stop. Cutter swung the car around the back of the station and got out.

When he pushed the wicket gate open, Longfield was waiting for him in the station house. Cutter stepped in and was hit by the smell.

'Careful where you stand, it's all over the floor; starts six feet after you're in.'

'Diesel?'

'A tankful,' said Longfield, pointing to the length of tubing that hung from the appliance. He became slightly cowed, flexing his fingers as he worked out how to proceed. 'Listen, John, I'm sorry about this, I really am. I was debating whether to call you when you drove past.'

'What's the big deal?'

'Well, it's government property to start with, but,' he gestured at the scene, 'it looks deliberate, don't you think? She didn't mean us to be able to save that house.'

'She?'

'Well.' Longfield's awkwardness increased. He chewed his lip for a second, rolled his eyes, avoiding Cutter's. 'It was Debbie, John – Mrs Cutter.'

'Deborah will do,' said Cutter, hiding his confusion and surprise. 'There is no Mrs Cutter.'

'Okay, fine. If that's how you want it.'

'That's how it is.'

Cutter took his cap off, hunkered down and took a good look under the appliance, to ascertain the full extent of the spill.

'The whole tank?'

Longfield raised a shutter, took a monkey wrench from a side locker and hit the fuel tank, producing a hollow galvanised boom.

'Less one jerrycan that's missing from the store. I'd say you'll find it in the Evans' house if you look.'

'You sure it was Deborah?'

'It's what I heard. She was the only one there, next to an empty jerry can. They pulled her away before she got burned herself.'

'Well,' said Cutter, 'at least it was put to good use.' He straightened. 'Thanks for letting me know.'

Longfield scratched his head.

'Is that it?'

'There's something else?'

'I don't know. I thought you might want a statement or, you know, in case you charge her. I mean, look at it. It's not right.'

'I could charge her, certainly. There's theft, unlawful entry, damaging government property, arson, man-slaughter, murder, concealment of a body, not reporting a death. I mean, take your pick.'

Longfield frowned, unsure what to do or say. Cutter took two steps closer to him.

'But I don't think we want to do that, do we? You were there last night, at the killing, and from what you say, and the smell of your overalls, at the burning. You think Deborah would forget to mention all that if she was in court?'

'I wasn't thinking.'

'That's why you fight fires and I fight crime. I think it would be better for all concerned if you got rid of the tube and had your mechanic fix that leak. Agree?'

'I could do that,' nodded Longfield, a smirk of understanding starting to develop. 'The old girl has been losing diesel recently. A worn seal, I'd guess. Must be it finally went last night. Some coincidence, hey?'

'Synchronicity.'

'Aye, that as well.'

'Right, I'm away, if you've nothing else.'

Murray Longfield, 9    Clifford Longfield, 11

*Seven years earlier*

Murray and Clifford Longfield tramped into the play-ground, sulking together in resignation as another school day began. They attended in matching donkey jackets, John Deere overalls and wellingtons, farm clothes that gave the impression their presence was temporary. Each held a duffle bag containing indoor shoes that didn't carry the reek of livestock.

Blood-born farmers and vociferous detesters of schol-arly education, they'd been convinced by their father that anything not learned with the hands would prove a false knowledge. They were already competent tractor drivers, hay-balers and mucker-outers. Much of this experience had been acquired in recent months of early-morning rises and pre-school chores. As their mum's illness worsened, Murray and Clifford had taken on her share of the farm work, willingly putting their hands to adult tasks. Their growing contribution corresponded with her deterioration and the increasing amount of time their dad had to dedicate to her needs. The washing of their overalls so the boys could be buried in comfort was the final thing she was able to do for herself.

They were the only children in the class who had ever killed anything larger than a spider or seen more blood than a nosebleed or a tooth loss. That autumn, their dad, John, who butchered what he farmed and much of what was reared nearby, had introduced his boys to the art of slaughter. Each had been instructed on how to plunge a knife deep into the brisket of a stunned pig to allow for the letting of the animal's blood. They had later watched as he had cut the pig's eyes out, rinsing them before putting them in the fridge overnight. Murray and Clifford brought the eyes to school for dissection. To the amazement of their classmates, they each rolled one around their mouth; a party trick learned from Dad. Connor Gardner puked. Robbie and Cameron Voar collapsed in a heap, slapping each other and laughing. Most of the boys turned away. The girls ran to the farthest reaches of the classroom. Dog Evans found the swirling of the eyes around their mouths hysterical. His laughter scared the others into silence, making the Longfields spit them back into the container.

Murray spat into the snow as they searched for Dog Evans. He was nowhere to be seen. Moving to where the boys were gathering, they turned their donkey-jacket collars against the building wind.

# 18

Driving against the peak-hour traffic, Shep and Rebecca left the anonymity of their suburban commuter estate. Using the ring road to bypass the city, Shep headed north with the feeling that they were leaving society behind. Rebecca was already half asleep as the last of the tall buildings retreated out of the rear window. He had often marvelled at how she couldn't stay awake for long on any mode of transport, regardless of noise or motion. He recalled sharing the joke, a long time ago now, when they had agreed that that was how she kept her good looks; travelling with him on business, waking up refreshed and hungry in a different town from the one they'd had breakfast in. He remembered driving the baby around the village so he would sleep: a good memory. Rebecca didn't have any.

They were soon travelling on open roads through lonesome country into the charred winter sunset. They would arrive in darkness, the same way they had left.

Four hours out of the city, two hours into the night and an hour since they had passed the last car, the road snaked down into the broad U of an enormous glacial valley. Shep squinted ahead and the corners of his mouth curled slightly. In the distance, the pinprick of familiar lights twinkled from a single building in the vast blackness that contained them. Without that beacon he could have been forgiven for believing that they were journeying as the last people on earth.

The isolated inn had been established over three hundred years ago to service the drovers taking their cattle to the markets of the south. Drifts of sheep had replaced the herds of cows, and tonight, woolly and stupid descendants of those initial drifts had chosen the road to sleep on and Shep was forced to slow down in order to steer around the clumps of dozing mutton.

At dips and bends the road disappeared from under them and his main beams ranged across the heather of the valley floor, capturing the bowed heads of deer, down from the steep sides for night feeding. He came to a halt once, to avoid and admire an enormous stag as it stood across the tarmac, from one side to the other. Imperious, it looked to have been waiting. Its flanks moved gently with each unhurried breath as it examined the car, unblinking and aloof, utterly convinced of its own place in the land-scape, considering theirs. Vapours drifted from its nostrils and threaded through its antlers as it weighed them up, as if it alone had the power to permit Shep and Rebecca to continue. Judgement passed, the beast flicked its ears and moved out of the glare. The road ahead was clear and straight. Ten minutes later, Shep allowed his bladder to relax as they pulled in to the buttery halos of the coach lanterns hanging from the gable end of the outbuildings.

He contemplated leaving her in the car, she looked so peaceful. He could be in and out before he knew it. But as he saw the jagged scar within her crow's feet twitch, he knew it was a bad idea, taking the chance of her waking alone in the dark.

A gentle shake roused her. She blinked and looked around as she came to.

'Where are we?'

'At the inn.' He leant across and wiped the corner of her mouth. 'You've got dribble.' He pulled his door handle. Rebecca checked her lipstick in the mirror as Shep got out and walked around the car.

Her big eyes were waiting for him when he opened her door. 'I don't want to.'

'Well, I'm afraid I need to. Come on.'

'Shep, please.'

'Please what?'

She didn't say anything.

'Rebecca, please what?'

She shrugged. He let go of her door and walked away, calling back to her, 'Should I bring you something out? I'm sure they'll still be doing bar snacks.'

The mere suggestion of being left alone was enough to make her button up and get out of the car. He looked back as she closed the door and started after him.

'Why are you being like this?'

'Like what?'

'Making me do things – this.' She gestured at the situation, the car, the inn, the night. 'It's not like you.'

'Rebecca, for God's sake, everything about *this*,' he mimicked her, 'it's something we have to do.'

He regretted the snap in his voice. He walked back and coddled her into him. With her forehead on his chest, her arms went around his waist; her black-gloved fingers interlocked.

'Shep, don't blaspheme, please.'

'I'm sorry, I didn't mean to.' He kissed the top of her head. 'Come on. I'm tired, I need the toilet and it hasn't been an easy day. Has it?'

She uncoupled and followed him into the inn.

When Shep came out of the porch toilet, she was still waiting for him. He opened the main door into the bar.

Inside, as had often been the case, he was surprised to see people. The summer ramblers had been replaced by the extreme hikers and the foolhardy, crowded around the open peat-fire in T-shirts, their outer garments of fleece and waterproof piled high on one chair or another. The far corner was occupied by a noisy group that he assumed had rented the bunkhouse attached to the inn: hunters, judging from their accents and their clothes, here to kill the deer he had been minded to appreciate. He sat Rebecca at the round table by the window with a radiator.

The barman extended a thick ham of a hand, barely contained by the sleeve of his fawn checked shirt.

'Shep. Good to see you,' he said, with genuine warmth. 'You've been a stranger to us.'

'Hello, Bill. It's good to see you too.'

'You've lost weight.'

'You haven't changed a bit.'

'More's the pity.'

Shaggy black hair crowned a face that shone from the effects of the weather and alcohol to such a degree that the large permanent spot on the end of his nose had little choice but to glow.

'How long has it been?'

'Must be a few years.'

'At least, I would say. What happened, was it your work?'

'Something like that: promotions, reshuffles, office politics, regional changes of responsibility, that kind of thing.'

'Sounds terrible, if you ask me; don't know how you do it. You're still keeping busy, though?'

'Oh, aye, bills to pay, obligations. You know how it is. Still got the nose to the grindstone. Just trying to keep close to home.'

'And the lady is?' said Bill, nodding across to Rebecca as she stood to remove her duffle coat.

'That's my wife,' said Shep, seeing her afresh, as though with Bill's attention. 'Rebecca.'

'Heavens, I'm not surprised you kept her a secret, you lucky sod.' Bill waved as Rebecca happened to look over, having placed her folded duffle on the deep windowsill. She found a smile for him. 'She's a smasher.'

'Always has been.'

'Here, what am I like?' said Bill, making to come out from behind the bar. 'She'll be freezing there. Let me get you two a seat closer to the fire. Bloody hunters spread out like they own the place sometimes, untidy sods.'

'No, no,' said Shep, waving for Bill to stay where he was. 'Please, don't disturb them. We're only in for one, just breaking the journey.'

'You're sure?'

'Absolutely.'

'Well, if you're sure. What'll it be?'

'A whisky and a brandy, thanks.'

'Back to the village, is it?'

'Aye.'

'And what takes you all the way out there?'

'Family. Our son.'

'Ach, that's good. He'll be pleased to see you, I would imagine. Enjoy your drinks.' Bill waved Shep's money away as he turned to the hunters, who were hailing from their end of the bar. 'Boys?'

Shep sat at the table with Rebecca, placing her brandy on the beer mat.

'Thank you,' she said. She moved the glass so that it sat in the centre of the mat, equidistant from each corner.

'Bill thinks you're beautiful.'

'That's nice of him to say so.'

'So do I.'

'I know.'

He touched his glass to hers before taking a sip.

'Did you come here often? You seem to know each other well.'

'Not really. It was just a natural place to stop after a long week on the road. Recharge the batteries before I got home.' Shep continued, encouraged as Rebecca raised her head and began to look around, taking an interest. 'I don't think you'd need to come in more than a couple of times, however infrequently, to become a regular. It's not like he has any locals. It's all passing trade, each customer a cold call.'

'And he's a good salesman?'

'Well, he got me and I know all the tricks.'

'I'm sure you do.'

Rebecca took the room in.

'I can see why you'd like it,' she said.

'How so?'

'It's simple: stone walls, stone floor, wooden furniture.'

'Function over form.'

'That sounds like John Cutter.'

'It's uncomplicated.'

'Yes, that's it. I can see how it would calm a man, especially when combined with alcohol.'

'You know me well.'

'Did you stop here after?'

'No. I never did,' said Shep. 'You needed me more.'

Rebecca drank from her glass, used a folded tissue to remove the lipstick and replaced it precisely where it had come from.

'Will you be okay,' she said, 'driving after drinking whisky?'

'I'll be fine. I'll take it easy; besides, it's not like I don't know the road. Matter of fact, I think I even recognised some of the deer we passed.'

Her smile for him was slight but it was honest and came with a look he would drive all day and all night for.

'Stop teasing. I was thinking more about the police, you know that. We don't want you losing your licence.'

'I wouldn't worry about it. It's only one. Besides, the next policeman we see will be John Cutter. What I've had to drink will be the last thing on that man's mind.'

The reminder of where they were headed took the life out of her face. She stilled her hand by wrapping it around the glass but she merely held on tight, unable to raise it to her lips. Shep took another sip.

It was more of a yelp than a scream; high-pitched

and loaded with shock: enough to silence the hubbub of the inn. She held her hand above the table, unable to take her eyes off the shard of glass that hung from the fleshy ball of her thumb, vibrating in tune with her pulse. Blood from the piercing flowed down it, dripping from its corner into what remained of the brandy, heavy drops dispersing like wet smoke rings. Continued dripping collided the rings and quickly disguised the spirit, the level rising in the glass until it reached the bottom of the break, where it trickled out, soaking into the perfectly positioned beer mat.

'Shite,' said Bill. 'Bloody glasses, they're always doing that.' He was at the table before they knew it, with a glass cloth for the wound. 'I think it's the washer myself, it weakens them. They move, no matter how I pack them.'

'No, no, no, no, stop,' someone called as Bill knelt and was poised with his indelicate grip. 'Let me take a look, please.'

The table was surrounded in an instant by a subtle conference of hikers who were doctors and an outer commotion of hunters drawn to the smell of blood and perfume and the sight of a wounded hind. The bleeding hand was held in the centre of this performance. Once agreement was reached, the doctor holding her hand, with a perfect bedside manner, said, 'Okay, you may want to close your eyes, or look away.'

Rebecca looked at Shep, no longer in the moment. Her lips moved.

'I'm sorry.'

'It's too late,' said Shep.

He watched her dissolve, deserted momentarily by the

support of her God and left alone. He sat still as she allowed herself to be comforted by Bill. Shep could tell he was already a little bit in love with her. She winced as the shard was removed and the hole was wiped with a clean handkerchief. Once the doctors were content there were no splinters left in the wound, the handkerchief was used to apply pressure and staunch the flow.

When the bandage was on and Rebecca had tried to dry her eyes as she thanked everybody, and the doctors became hikers once more, following the hunters back to their drinks, Bill let his arm slide from her shoulders, where it no longer felt appropriate.

'I feel bad,' he said. 'I've suspected that washer of doing this for a while. Honestly, you can hear them rattling against each other when it's on, you know what I mean?'

Rebecca put her good hand on Bill's forearm to quiet him.

'It wasn't the glass,' she said. 'It was me. I had hold too tight.'

'Don't be ridiculous, girl. I won't have you blaming yourself.'

'I thought it would stop the shaking. I didn't want to embarrass myself, being somewhere Shep was known.' She looked Bill right in the eye, talking as though Shep was no longer there. 'He's been so good to me. I don't want him to be ashamed of me, ever.'

Bill stalled, unsure, no longer confident his bluff bar-keep persona could carry the day.

'Come on now,' he said. 'As if anybody could be ashamed of you. And this is a lot of fuss about a broken glass, wouldn't you say, Shep?'

Shep was focused on the remains of her drink, still stunned by her apology, when his trance was broken by Bill's question. When he glanced up, he could see that Bill was asking for help. Shep leant forward, a hand on Rebecca's knee. Bill leant in to meet him, needing an explanation.

'Like Rebecca said, it's not about the glass. Our son died. Yesterday, we think. We were only informed this morning.'

'Oh, Jesus,' said Bill, the power leaving his voice. 'I'm so sorry.'

'Thank you. It's why we're here, why we're going back to the village. We shouldn't have come in. It was a bad idea.'

'No. Not at all.'

Shep sat back. Rebecca took her hand from Bill's arm. When she did, he had already begun to relax, the way Shep knew he would. Grief was reason and explanation enough for any kind of behaviour. Knowing Rebecca had lost her son obliged him to forgive her for making him uncomfortable. The tears, the intensity, the strangeness of the girl were all rendered understandable by her grief.

'I'm glad you felt you could, Shep. You'll always be welcome here, you know that, the both of you, whatever the circumstances. Though I can't see them ever being worse.'

He lifted the glass and swept the debris from the table into the cloth.

'Let me replace this,' he said. 'I'm sure you could use it. I know I would. Just give me a minute.'

He caught the drips in the bowl of his free hand as he

carried the sweepings behind the bar and through into the kitchen.

'Come on,' said Shep.

He helped Rebecca to her feet and wrapped her duffle around her, pulling the collar up to shield her, hoping Bill would know to stay in the back and give them enough time. He didn't want the awkwardness to be increased with goodbyes.

Outside, beneath the rancour of the crows in the high spruce branches, he held Rebecca close until she had stopped trembling. Over her shoulder he saw Bill's huge fists draw the curtains and was grateful for the privacy.

Hamilton Walker, 7

*Seven years earlier*

When Hamilton Walker ducked into the wigwam, he held a penlight torch in one hand, the beam of which was trained on the contents of the other. Robbie, Cameron and Jack leant in to see the fallen bird. A red ring and a grey metal ring were crimped on to one rigid leg. Both feet gripped an invisible perch. Its head rolled with the movement of Hamilton's fingers.

'It's a bird,' he said.

'Is it asleep?' said Cameron.

'Dead.'

'That's a shame.'

'But still pretty.'

'Yes,' said Hamilton, 'it is.'

As Hamilton examined the bird, he was already working out how best to turn it into a drawing. He saw it as lines, strokes, finger smudges and cross-hatch shading.

'What kind is it?' asked Jack Todd.

'I don't know. We should ask Norrie, he'll know.'

They left the wigwam like a funeral cortège.

Standing with the older boys, Norrie only turned around when Cameron pulled at the back of his jacket. The instant he saw the bird he was interested, bending down for a closer look.

'Do you know what that is?' said Hamilton.

'It's a snow bunting.'

'Why? It isn't white.'

'They only go white in the summer. This is his winter plumage.'

The younger boys looked with new appreciation.

'It can change colour?'

'Yes.'

'How did it die?'

'I couldn't say. Maybe it's old, come to the end of its life cycle.'

'It doesn't look old.'

'It's pretty.'

'Yes, it is.'

'Is it the last one?'

'I wouldn't think so. Keep a watch out, they usually fly in flocks.'

'What?'

'Groups, big families.'

'Is he a daddy?'

'Probably.'

'Will his children be sad?'

'I don't know if a bird can be sad.'

The boys didn't know what to make of this statement. It stemmed their questions. With a quick ruffle of the nape feathers and one final look, Norrie turned back to the older boys' conversation.

'Let's show Maggie,' said Robbie.

'Why?' said Hamilton.

'Because.'

Robbie and Cameron dragged Hamilton across the

playground, the bird held to his chest between two possessive hands. Maggie was waiting for them when they arrived, a few steps away from the other girls and their dozing charge.

'What's the matter, boys?'

Robbie and Cameron poked Hamilton, urging him to show Maggie. Reluctantly he held the bird out.

'Aagh, poor birdie.'

'It's a snow bunting,' said Jack.

'It's dead,' said Robbie.

'Can we bury it?' said Cameron.

Hamilton yanked the bird tight to his body.

'I know you like it, Hammy,' said Maggie, bending to his height and adopting her grown-up tone. 'But I think that would be best, don't you, before it starts to smell and all the beasties come out of it? Why don't you bury it under the holly bush, so you can see the grave from where you sit?'

'That's a good idea,' said Jack. 'Just by your window, it couldn't be closer.'

'Okay.'

'Nobody else touch it except Hammy,' said Maggie. 'It's his bird. And you be sure to wash your hands as soon as school opens, and no biting your nails or scratching your face; there'll be germs, okay?'

Hamilton nodded. Maggie went back to the girls. He followed the younger boys to the holly bush, regretting that they had made him show Maggie his bird.

They cleared the snow with their feet and used sticks to scratch a shallow burial place in the frozen ground. Hamilton put the bunting in the bottom, scraped soil over it and stood up. He pressed his palms together and closed his eyes, his head slightly forward as his lips moved in silent prayer. Robbie and Cameron followed suit, each looking at the other through half-opened eyes and with a slight sideways tilt of the head, not sure when it was over. Jack Todd left them to walk over to the older boys.

## 19

The final few hours of single track were still so familiar to Shep it was as if he'd only been away days, not years. Glancing at Rebecca as he drove, it struck him how few times they had made this journey together, in either direction. Usually he'd been alone, tired and leaving or tired and coming home. Initially he'd found peace amongst the valley floors and along loch shores, come to enjoy the hairpin bends over narrow bridges that spanned boiling streams of mountain meltwater, the loch-end collections of timber fishing huts and upturned boats commanding views right down the length of the waterways. He'd befriended the ruined houses and lone chimney stacks, stark against the skyline, set back from what had never been their main road and now only accessible by foot. Each lonely assembly of stones had become a welcome ticking-off of distance travelled, of fewer miles to go. The longer they lived in the village, the more he related to their isolation.

What little certainty there was about his homecomings had evaporated after the accident. Each time he got back, he would find Rebecca's state of mind a little more unhinged, a little harder to repair. Their son took to vanishing for days or isolating himself within the house, as if he knew he was the cause of her upset. Shep spent his weekends balancing Rebecca's eggshell sensitivities and trying to coax their boy out of his compulsion to hide. He said he felt safe when nobody could see him. It got so that Shep knew where he would be the moment he walked through the door. If he was in his room, Rebecca would be on the sofa with the fire on, in all weathers, reading or watching television; a regular evening. There would be food in the oven. Shep would hug Rebecca, give her flowers, or shockolates – so called because she always acted surprised – and say he was hungry. Then, while she busied in the kitchen, he would go up to sit on the landing and talk to his boy through the gap he allowed in the door.

'Hi.'

'Hi.'

'Everything okay?'

The boy would nod.

'You look lonely.'

'I'm the only child.'

'Are you going to come and join us?'

'No, I'm fine.'

'You sure you won't come down? You must be hungry.'

'No.'

'I'd like to see you.'

'Why?'

'I've been away all week.'

'Can I come with you?'

'What was that?'

'On Monday.'

'All week?'

'Yes.'

'But what about your mum? Do you think it's right I

should leave her alone, without a man in the house?'

After a long pause, he said, 'No.'

'Good. Your mum needs a man in the house to look after her.'

'I know.'

'Shake on it.'

Through the gap a man's hand would grip a youth's hand in the space permitted by the security chain he had asked Shep to bring home from his travels. Shep had assumed he wanted to put it on the front door and saw it as a reaction to the way Rebecca had been treated. The boy wanted to protect his mother. He was disappointed and upset that weekend when he came home and found access to his son's room now governed by his son.

'You don't have to be on your own.'

'It's easier.'

Shep had no comeback.

'Dad?'

'Yeah.'

'Go downstairs.'

'Why?'

'You can still make her laugh. I like listening when you talk.'

'Why don't you come down and talk with us.'

'Sorry's not a conversation.'

His hand would slip out of Shep's. The door would be closed. And again, Shep had no recourse.

When Shep told her their son liked being alone, it was all she needed to hear.

'He's nearly sixteen.'

'He is.'

'He can look after himself.'

'Pretty much.'

'So?'

'Rebecca? What are you saying?'

'We could leave.'

'No, we couldn't.'

'I need to find peace, Shep.'

It was the start of the attrition.

On the days the boy had gone out, yet to return from wherever he went, Rebecca would be pacing the ground floor from curtain to curtain, arm's-length twitching, her left hand worrying the rosary she had taken to carrying at all times. The anticipation of the boy's return prevented relaxation, conversation or eating and frequently ended up causing arguments between Shep and Rebecca.

Shep preferred it when he was in, but it got to the point where the boy retreated to the point of not being there. The weekends became Shep and Rebecca again, and if their son wasn't mentioned, Rebecca wouldn't shake or shout or cry. Shep tried to accept this, but saw it as a failure on his part. Once, angry with her instability and the boy's absence, he kicked the door through, rending the chain from the woodwork, and made him come downstairs, physically dragging him. They all sat around the table miserable while the food went cold until Shep said he could go.

It was the last time Shep forced him down. It was the last time Shep wanted him at the table.

'I made him go.'

Shep was still considering the waste of three uneaten meals, the cost of meat, the absence of family.

'Shep.'

'What?'

'I made him go, to his room. I hit him.'

'What?'

'He laughed at me.'

'You hit him because he laughed at you?'

'No. He laughed because I hit him. He won.'

'What the fuck are you talking about?'

'Don't swear, Shep. Please.'

'Speak plainly, Rebecca. I'm exhausted and in no mood.'

He paid heed as Rebecca gathered herself. He could tell it was an effort and already didn't want to hear what was coming.

'I'd showered,' she said. 'I was drying myself.' She struggled to control her emotions.

'What? Was he watching?'

'I was drying my legs.'

She bent forward and swept her hands down to her ankles, suggesting the position she was in. She appeared on the verge of hysteria and Shep went to hold her, but she pushed him away. The rim of her eye patch was damp from tears.

Shep had underestimated what was to come.

'He put his fingers in.' She squirmed in her seat, repulsed. 'I can still feel them.' Her voice was shrill and pained and shamed.

'Rebecca?'

'He had it out, rubbing it.'

When Shep got to the bedroom, the window was open and his room was empty.

On Monday morning, Shep took Rebecca with him, leaving their son to fend for himself. On their return, they saw he hadn't needed them. The house was clean. A meal was prepared. He wasn't there. He didn't come home.

The next weekend, he was sixteen. Rebecca thought she'd found her peace.

But she was suffering tonight. Although she had tried to go back to sleep, she had been writhing all over the seat. Her hand hurt. Blood had seeped through the bandage and stained the bindings across her palm. She was increasingly fretful the closer they got. Shep wanted her to find peace, even if he couldn't. He felt guilty for being disappointed that the death had not been confirmed. That they both wished their only son dead brought no pride. Which was as well, Shep having often been a stranger to pride.

How Finnegan had acquired the photographs, Shep could only guess. Images Shep considered tame that made use of his physique and looks in a time of need. Maybe it was somebody in the village; more likely another priest. But Finnegan used the evidence of Shep's only sortie into pornography to demonise him and his family. He undertook house visits to everyone who had lost a child. He used these visits to share the images. Scrolled in his hand, the tawdry pages took on the significance of religious text. They became proof, as Finnegan forged a direct link between Shep's shrouded past and the boy's strangeness, insisting his 'condition' was God's comment on Shep's carnality. He used grief to galvanise the injustice surrounding the boy's survival.

Shep felt the change in the way people dealt with him. Initially he assumed their avoidance to be a manifestation of their pain. His drop in local sales was to be expected. Weeks later, when still nobody spoke to him or answered his calls, he knew something else was going on. Only when he cornered Nugget did he find out what was behind the silence; that he and Rebecca had 'brought it upon themselves'.

Bursting into Finnegan's house, he'd half throttled him as he warned him off Rebecca. His thumbprints could be seen on the priest's windpipe the following Sunday, when Finnegan damned Rebecca for being the receptacle of Shep's seed. Mary Magnal had walked Rebecca home. She kept apologising for Father Finnegan's words. Shep had told her to go away without thanking her or inviting her in.

By now, Mary was the only parishioner who still tolerated Finnegan's visits. Initially welcoming them as a chance to share a grief that might otherwise overwhelm, families had come to dread them. He refused to let them stop grieving. He obsessed over their loss. John Cutter had been the first to throw him out. Others had quickly followed suit. There was talk of him losing his mind. Mary Magnal, the only single mother in the village, was the first to conceive after the tragedy. Shep had pointed the finger at Finnegan.

# 20

Wittin searched for Deborah. He tried her lodgings. When she didn't answer, he entered, calling her name. Her clothes from the night before were in the washing machine. The fresh smell of bathing lingered in the room. A damp towel hung from the bathroom door. Condensation ran down the window. A bronze pubic hair shone wet in the bottom of the bath. The thought of her naked and washing aroused him.

In the bedroom, the pictures of Jenny took his desire away. Perfume and hair products lay on the dresser. The idea of her cleaning up to go out and find another man drove him to comb the village once more for her. She hadn't been seen in the tavern or any of the bars. She wasn't on streets, down lanes, alleys or dead ends. Hours passed; night fell. He had looked everywhere he knew and was mightily pissed off with being dismissed, told he was wasting his time or that she might not want to be found.

The car that passed him that night on its way down Main Street stopped outside the hotel. He held back to observe. After talking to Cutter, he assumed the couple that got out had to be Dog's parents. Seconds later, they had been welcomed into the hotel and the street was empty. Tomorrow, John Cutter would lie to them and gauge their reactions. He would show them the cremated corpse and tell them it was their son. If they believed him, there would have been no murder. Cutter and the village would carry on as if legitimate justice had been done. Wittin retreated to his church.

The heating had been on all day. It was oppressive. Wittin drank two bottles of holy wine on the altar steps, tossing the first empty at an imagined congregation. It bounced off the faithless, rattled between pews and rolled out into the aisle. He pushed the second over in the early hours as he slumped onto the carpet, his head on Deborah Cutter's pillow.

# 21

It was coming on to one in the morning when Shep parked the car. His shoulders were solid with tension and pain knifed through his muscles as his hands slid to the bottom of the wheel. He yawned as he looked across at Rebecca.

'We're here, baby.'

Rebecca stared into the middle distance, refusing to focus upon the village she had once craved and now despised.

'It hasn't changed,' she said.

'It's night, you can't tell.'

'I can feel.'

He didn't want to agree with her. It couldn't be the same. Time had to have healed things, even slightly. What had driven them away couldn't have survived this long. It had to be blunted at least; the edges rounded so that they didn't catch on every element of daily life. It wasn't the same. Shep thought it was worse but told himself he was just worn out.

'Do you want to drive down to the house, see what's left?'

'What are we going to see?'

'What do you want to see?'

'I think I'd rather be blind than see any of this again.'

'Please don't say that, even in jest, Rebecca.'

He saw from the look she gave him how far away from jesting she was.

Shep walked around to the passenger side. He opened her door, helped her out. Rebecca was instinctively drawn to the church as Shep lifted their luggage from the back seat. She saw that lights were on inside.

'Long drive?'

They turned to see a young man stepping from the hotel doorway in shirtsleeves.

'Please let me take that.'

'You're okay, I'll manage,' said Shep. 'It's only two bags, but thank you.'

'My pleasure. Please.' He held the door open and ushered them inside.

'I'm Glen Masson. I run the hotel with Sally, my wife. She's sleeping. Here's your key.'

'Thank you.'

'You're on the half-landing. Can I get you anything? Soup, toast, a hot drink, a nightcap?'

The new owner had no idea who they were.

'Thank you, no. We appreciate the offer but I think we're fine, aren't we?' Rebecca nodded in agreement. Shep saw that she had covered her bandaged hand with her scarf. 'And thank you, for waiting up.'

'You're welcome,' he said. 'But it's not unusual. You'd be surprised how many people misjudge the time it takes to get up here.'

'The single-track roads.'

'Exactly.'

'Breakfast any time,' said Glen Masson, pushing

through the door behind the reception desk. 'No need to get up early. Goodnight.'

'Goodnight.'

He left them alone in the calm of the foyer.

'Nice man,' said Shep, guiding Rebecca to the staircase.

'It won't last. This place will get him too.'

'Come on,' he put his arm around her waist, 'you need to sleep.' He continued as they climbed, though without any response from Rebecca. He may as well have been talking to himself, reminding himself of why they had left the city in the first place to come here. 'There was a time that this was the only place in the world you wanted to live. It was isolated and therefore safe, an ideal place for bringing children up. And nobody knew anything about me; remember? It was perfect. A fresh start.'

They had a corner room. It was clean and modern. From the windows they could see the church and the school.

'Well now,' said Shep, putting the bags on the bed. 'Not what I expected.'

Rebecca went straight to the curtains and closed them. She hung her coat in the wardrobe, took her cotton nightgown from the top of the case and undressed, folding her worn clothes into a neat pile. As she slipped her nightgown over her head, letting it drop down her body, Shep sat in the armchair next to the window to hide his erection, which he felt was inappropriate. She took the toiletries bag into the en suite. He watched her in the mirror as she cleaned her teeth, slowly, without any enthusiasm. Her reflection vanished and he heard her on the toilet, then flushing, the running of taps and the unfolding of towels as she dried her hands. When she came out, she turned the bathroom light off. The hum of the extractor fan continued. She pulled the sheets back, climbed into bed and pulled them up to her chin.

'We ruined it,' she said, 'didn't we?'

'I'm sorry?'

'We ruined the dream.'

He bent to untie his laces so she couldn't see the weariness on his face. He wanted to shake her hard and clear his mind of the unsaid.

'We can't be blamed for everything.' He eased his shoes off. 'It was a collision of events, some outwith our control, others, well, we could have dealt with differently.'

'Shep. Why have you never told me I was a bad mother?'

'I resent you asking that, Rebecca. It forces me to admit that I was a bad father.'

'You tried in a way I didn't. Kept trying.'

'You were always my priority.'

'Could you look at me?'

'I don't think I can at the moment.'

He stayed where he was until she could no longer bear to wait, had turned on her side and fallen asleep. When he lifted the quilt and climbed in beside her, he had aged. He kissed her, lay back and closed his eyes; dead beat.

He awoke during the night. The bedside light was on. His face was wet. He turned to see Rebecca watching him from her pillow. A fine tear trail ribboned from one eye down into the other, across the bridge of her nose and onto the stained cotton pillowcase. Beneath the blankets her fingers meshed with his. He wondered what she had been thinking as she watched him cry.

'Are we bad people, Shep?'

He didn't answer.

'To think what we think, does it mean we're damned?'

'What we think?' He rolled onto his side to face her. 'If you're considering damnation, Rebecca, consider what's been done.'

He looked at her.

'I believe that at best I'm weak. Right now, I don't feel my best. Mostly, I'm ashamed. That's hard. It's my fault, though. I can't blame anybody else for things I did, or failed to do.'

'We did.'

'My actions were my own, Rebecca, yours your own. Shame isn't lessened by its sharing.'

He felt her fingers slide from between his.

He turned the light off.

He lay awake until morning.

Rebecca claimed not to be hungry so Shep took breakfast alone. He had black coffee, soft-poached eggs on toast with English mustard, more coffee and a sweet pastry. He took his time, enjoying the peace of the dining room. He felt lighter when she came down.

It was as though the crater had consumed the house.

Shep held Rebecca as they stood on the lip looking down at John Cutter. She was wrapped in her duffle, sunglasses against the low reluctant sun.

'I wish it was different,' said John Cutter.

'What?'

'Our meeting again, the reason.'

'Wishing it was different goes back a long way, John,

longer each day. Just tell us what happened.'

After meeting Shep's stare for a few moments, John Cutter continued.

'I don't know for sure how it started,' he said. 'Still looking into that.'

'The fire service didn't attend?'

'No. Nobody called them.'

'That says more about you than him.'

'I'd agree.'

'How sure are you, John?' said Rebecca.

Cutter wished she'd take her glasses off; wanted to see if her eyes were as desperate as her voice.

'I'm satisfied he was at home.'

'But you can't be certain?' said Shep.

'He always was,' said Cutter. 'I'm equally satisfied that nothing or nobody survived the fire. Some remains were found, more than likely your boy's.'

He pointed to the tarpaulin. Rebecca wept, over-wrought, stepping from foot to foot like some strange bird, her arms flailing. Shep tightened himself around her, compressed her and held on to stop her falling into the crater. He saw himself in her sunglasses as she spoke.

'It's over, Shep. He's gone. I want to leave, now; please, can we go?'

But Shep could smell the truth. It was a sense he prided himself on. He studied Cutter, arms crossed, standing tall in his police uniform, looking somewhere else, and he knew.

'What's wrong, John?'

Cutter was unprepared for the question and made no further attempt to cover up.

'Quite a lot, Shep. But I'd say it's best you accept what I tell you.'

'Best for who?'

'All of us in the long run. Nobody's coming back.'

'You're sure?' said Rebecca.

'I'm afraid I am, Rebecca.'

'Listen to him, Shep.'

'I don't know if I can.'

She took her sunglasses off. 'Please. For everybody, like he said.'

He wiped her cheeks clean.

The edge of John's voice was dulled. 'I can't help you any more than I have, Shep. There are other people to think about. I feel responsible.'

Wittin woke up. Slaver streaked his jowl. Rubbing his face brought some life back. The first thing his eyes lit on was the bottle in the aisle. It was upright. Beyond it, light slanted through the open door. It felt cooler. He looked at his watch. It was almost noon. John Cutter had told his lie.

Shuffling into the vestry, he broke the seal on another bottle and sucked out a curer. Upturning the church stationery box, he took paper and a black marker pen.

Standing in a doorway, hidden from view, Wittin watched the car in the reflection of the shop window. They were the only people in the hotel; it had to be them. The reaction of the man as he took the note from the car window left no doubt in Wittin's mind. He watched him as he sat down to smoke. He intended waiting for Mr Evans to finish his cigar and go back into the hotel.

But when the man was distracted by the arrival of Sally, Wittin took the opportunity to cross over Main Street and head out to the old school grounds.

The scrap of paper was tucked beneath the windscreen wiper. Shep looked up and down Main Street: not a soul in sight. The day was already losing its light. The air was grey and carried the taste of ash. He retrieved the paper. He checked again as he unfolded it, sure somebody was watching. He read the message, expecting more of the vile insults that had forced them to leave. He didn't look up again for many seconds. He absorbed the four words printed in black marker – GO TO THE SCHOOL.

He reached into the car, opened the glove compartment and pulled out a new cigar. Crumpling the cellophane into his pocket, he used the guillotine on his key ring to cut across the cone. Sitting on the hotel steps, he put the cigar into his mouth and puffed each time he turned it above the lighter's flame. When the end was evenly lit and it began to draw, he took a mouthful of smoke, enjoying the flavour, keeping it in longer than usual, feeling calmed by it. He pulled his jacket close as he let it go. He wondered if he should show Rebecca the note. He looked at it again.

He folded the paper when he heard the hotel door opening behind him.

'I'd say you're enjoying that.'

It was the clear voice of Sally, the girl who had served him breakfast while her husband Glen had slept on. He wasn't ready for Rebecca yet. He slipped the note into his inside pocket.

'Everything okay?'

'Yes,' he said. 'I am. Thank you.'

'Almost makes me want to try,' she said, indicating the cigar.

Shep held it out to her.

'Almost. Got through my teens without succumbing; be a shame to now.'

'Good for you.'

She came and sat on the step next to him, close enough that he could smell her. It was a good smell. She rolled her chunky polo-neck collar up against the cold.

'It's been quiet,' she said.

'Isn't it always?'

'No. Not on a Sunday. We've worked hard, managed to get a regular local trade ticking over, people coming in for coffees and pastries and the like, spending the morning reading the papers or talking. Sunday evenings they come and enjoy the last of the weekend. You'd be surprised.'

'No, I can see why. It's nice what you've done with the lounge, tasteful. Not like something I'd have expected to find here.'

'Thank you.'

'And breakfast was delicious.'

'You're welcome.' Leaning forward, her arms folded across her knees, she scanned the street, loose red waves moving across her shoulder with the movement of her head.

'No one at all. Must be something to do with the other night.'

Shep scratched the stubble on his chin, waited a few seconds.

'What happened the other night?'

'Not sure really. There was a fire, that's for sure. I could see sparks and smoke from here. Before that, I'm not sure.'

'You don't sound very sure about much.'

She smiled at him. He smiled back, taken by the clear whites of the girl's eyes and the small gap between her two front teeth.

'We're still seen as new, so we were excluded, or maybe not invited. I'm not sure.' She giggled. 'It has to do with the history of the place, though, I can sense that.' She looked at him. 'Do you know about …'

'I'm aware.'

He could tell that she'd wanted to tell him all about the accident at the school and he liked her and wished he hadn't taken the wind out of that sail.

'It's what the village is famous for.'

'I guess,' she said. 'It will change, though.'

'But there will always be an anniversary.'

'Yeah. I guess.'

'Tell me,' he said. 'Do you think a village can ever recover from such a history?'

'It's got to.'

'You banking on it?'

She nodded, rubbing her shins to generate some heat.

'The rawness dies with the people who feel it,' she said. 'Surely?'

'Or they leave and take it with them.'

'That's true as well, of course.'

'And bring it back.'

She turned and looked at him for a good few seconds.

'Is that why you're here?'

'The history? Yes, that's why we're here.'

A moment later, she put her hand on his arm and gave it a gentle squeeze, before standing and going back inside. He tingled beneath the touch of her half-understanding. It was all he could do not to weep.

Back in the hotel room, Rebecca was already packing their bags. She threw the car keys onto the bed as she read the note.

'Did you write this?'

'Rebecca.'

She pushed the paper back at him.

'Be honest with me.'

She went to the window. Beyond her, Shep could see the tips of the trees that grew in the school grounds. The moon was already high.

'I don't want to go.'

'Why?'

'There's nothing there.'

Shep held the note up.

'Somebody wants us to go there.'

'Why?'

'Maybe they want to help.'

'Here?'

'Somebody feels bad. Don't you sense it? You saw how John was.'

Rebecca lay down and pulled the counterpane over herself. Shep sat in the chair beside the bed. He leant low and close. Her face was still a feast. She was too beautiful for the boy to have been her fault.

'Rebecca, something isn't right.'

'What if he left the note?' she said.
'So you agree with me?'
She didn't answer straight away.
'I'm scared. He'll hate us.'
'He'd be right to.'
She nodded.
'Do you want me to go alone?'
'What do you mean?'
'I could leave you here; lock the door.'

*Seven years earlier*

The ground had been disturbed. Crouching, Kerr Munson poked at the snow bunting's grave with one of the loose twigs amongst the leaves that had been scraped aside. The bird was gone. He thought he could make out paw prints, a fox maybe. Standing to look beyond the bush, he was surprised to see larger footprints in the snow, not as fresh but recent. They didn't lead to the bush and the empty grave. They looked to come from the edge of the school field, from away beneath the drift building against the fence. They led to the school, to the window Hamilton sat by. The sill was swept clear of snow. Somebody had climbed in or out of the window. Kerr Munson wrote down all he saw. Closing his notebook, he made his way to the group of boys where Hamilton Walker was standing.

*Did you take the bird?* he wrote on a back page.

Hamilton looked confused. Kerr pointed. Hamilton shook his head, no.

'It was dead.'

*It's gone*, wrote Kerr.

'Really?' said Hamilton as he looked across at the bush. Before Kerr Munson could write another question, he was distracted. Jonny and Alice arrived at school, hand in hand. He went to the front of his notebook again, even though the wind and snow made it hard to write at all.

Jonny Raffique made a visible play of being Alice Corggie's protector as they walked through the school gate that final morning. Some of the smaller ones hid nervous laughter, but Jonny saw looks of admiration and envy on the faces of others. Alice gripped his arm.

'I don't see him,' she said.

'Me neither.'

'Should I stay with you?'

'No need.'

Her hold relaxed.

'Come and stand with me if he comes,' said Jonny.

'Okay.'

Alice let go and headed over to Jean and Jenny.

Jonny walked over to where the bunch of boys were in deep discussion. Kerr used a finger to keep his place in his notebook and joined the boys standing around Jonny. Jonny was always interesting and they hadn't run out of things to ask him yet. Kerr had a list of Jonny's favourite television programmes, the strange names of the candy he used to eat, the games he'd play and even some names and nicknames of his old classmates. Over recent weeks he had talked about gangs and neighbourhoods and they had hung on his every word. All except Dog Evans, who continued to hide his shared admiration of Juan Raffique, America in general and California in particular behind growls and a threatening posture designed to maintain a distance between them. Jonny was happy with this distance. At the same time it was obvious to them he was not scared of Dog Evans. He carried his past with him and they could sense his fears were of another magnitude altogether.

The gravity of his past was consolidated for them on their final day when he joined their compact, penguin-like cluster. Even before he arrived he could hear them, trying to butt in, earnestly trying to get their say about what they were going to do when they were older. Jonny listened.

'I shall,' said Calvin Struan, protesting at their sniggering. 'Just like father. All the Struans do their duty. It's a matter of honour.'

'What is?' said Jonny.

Fraser turned to him. 'Calvin says he's going to be a soldier.'

'Cool,' said Jonny.

Calvin was delighted.

'And what about you?'

'I want to work in a baker's,' said Fraser Blades, 'be warm and wear a suit.'

'Like me?' said Calvin Struan, mistaking it for a compliment.

'No,' said Fraser, 'not like you.'

'I'd like to be taller and stronger,' said Connor Gardner, 'so people stop putting me into bags and I can be a fireman.'

Norrie Storrie blew through his fingers. 'I want a nice job, but I don't know what, just something warm.'

'Tell me about it,' said Jonny Raffique.

'I know,' said Fraser. 'It's hard being a builder. You gets loads of money but you're cold and wet and dirty all the time. I might save up for a racing car.'

'I'm going to teach,' said Jack Todd. Nobody doubted him.

All eyes turned to the Longfields, next in line.

'What?' they said.

Murray and Clifford Longfield were amused by the possibility of doing anything other than the continued running of Longfield Farm. It was beyond their ken to imagine anything else, even racing cars, fire engines or being a soldier. They were farmers, overalls were their uniform and animal husbandry was their calling.

Likewise, Heavy Bevy was a child butcher; the village butcher in waiting. He stole a glance across the yard at Lucy Livingstone and toyed with the notion of pie-based wealth.

Kerr Munson wrote down all they said and nobody asked what he wanted to be. Kerr didn't write down what Jonny Raffique said. His hand trembled and his pen hung over the page as he joined the other boys gazing at Jonny. They'd expected something special when they'd asked him what he wanted to do when he grew up. It was no surprise to them that his reply made construction, racing cars and fire engines redundant. But still it was a surprise.

'I'm going back to Sausalito to kill my dad, so me and my mom can go home. I want to feel warm again.'

It was a career path they couldn't compete with: revenge. The damp and the cold of the day passed through their heavy boots and padded jackets into their blood. Coils of breath bound them. Connor Gardner loved his dad; he nearly cried but fought the tears in his attempt to grow up. He heard the girls laughing and wished himself still across the playground with them.

Jonny's vocation spread around the school.

What Jonny Raffique couldn't know was that he had planted the thought of parental murder, an altogether separate matricide, in the minds of his classmates, Clifford and Murray Longfield. They exchanged a look and understood. It struck them as the perfect solution.

The Longfields' home life had changed. Their mum's smile had lost most of its light. Dad's sadness never went away. Sometimes he broke down while he was working. He tried to hide it from the boys, but they saw. Clifford, being the eldest, tried to cheer and protect Murray. Murray wouldn't allow it, throwing his brother's arm from his shoulder each time he made an attempt to console him.

During the late spring, after the first calves, when it began, their mum and dad had sat them down and explained everything to them as carefully as they could, but the boys didn't really comprehend. As summer had drawn to a close and their mum had changed and been confined to a wheelchair, they found it hard to look at her and took any chance at all to be out of the house. They were angry with her, always sitting, not playing any more, unhappy. Ashamed, they made themselves scarce when friends or neighbours came to call. They hated Dr Corggie because he couldn't fix their mum. They hated the priest, Father Finnegan, for his useless praying and for holding on to their mum for too long. They hated their dad's cooking. Intuitively, the boys knew their dad was a good man. He had done nothing wrong for God to send Mum the disease as a punishment. It was easier when their mum had to stay in her bed and the door could be closed and they could remember her as she used to be.

She had been a tree surgeon, fit and strong, taller than their dad. Now she shook, her hands never still. It was impossible to picture them in control of a chainsaw. Sometimes she looked scared. Mostly she looked at her sons. Helpless when she had to be fed, mortified when she had to be cleaned she cried. Dad held her tight, until she was almost still.

The look between the brothers that morning as the other children gazed at Jonny was a rare moment of agreement. It would be a mercy killing. It would be for Mum. Clifford wondered if they should get Dad to help.

# 22

Shep drove down Main Street. He passed Munson's. The paintwork and the gold lettering on the shopfront hadn't changed. The window displays looked like they hadn't changed; jars of sweets on one side of the door, displays of proprietary medicines and toiletries on the other. The medicines had been put in the window not long after the accident to replace the children's toys that had lost their market and come to look distasteful.

Turning right at the bottom, he followed the left-hand sweep of the road around the marsh for the quarter-mile it took to reach the circular turning area at the dead end that was created when the entrance into the school grounds had been closed. He kept his attention to the right-hand side of the road, not wanting to look across the marsh. This forced him to take in the backs of houses that he passed. They looked to him to be long sealed up, rejected and forgotten, which saddened him. He felt he was a naturally optimistic person, despite it all.

As a salesman, his knocking on these doors, and being invited in through most of them, had been his introduction to many of the villagers, years before he and Rebecca had moved here. The first time she had accompanied him, curious to see his favourite destination, she had left him to conduct his business while she spent the afternoon hours investigating, walking up and down the handful of streets a dozen times at least. He had a good day; made some money and finished early. He waited for her at the car, parked in almost the same place he sat now, completing his paperwork so that it wouldn't hang over into the weekend. When Rebecca had finally come into view, it was little more than a saunter that brought her closer to him. She handed him all that was left of her ice cream cone, the last inch, a biscuit nipple of cold milk, for which he thanked her. She leant back with him, half sitting on the bonnet of the car, gazing out over the lush summer green of the marsh, where myriad flowers produced pinpricks of dancing colour: yellows, blues and pinks.

'Shep,' she said, 'I think we should come and live here. No, I think we need to.'

'I knew you'd like it,' he said.

'It feels special.'

'I think it's the fact that it's at the end of the road. You have to come here, if you see what I mean. You can't pass through or happen upon the place by accident.'

'It's a destination.'

'Precisely. Somewhere to arrive.'

He could see she had already made up her mind.

She pointed to a large grey bird that had revealed itself by moving. 'What's that? It's enormous.'

'That's a heron, and if I'm not mistaken, the thing wriggling in its beak is a frog. Whoops,' he said as the heron jerked its head. 'Was a frog. Do you think it'll kick all the way down?'

'Ugh, Shep, don't,' she said, waving her arms and dancing on the spot, her face creased in horror. 'That's disgusting.'

He grabbed her and flicked his tongue repeatedly against the skin in the crook of her neck, and she squealed and jumped up and ran around the car with her head pulled in and her hands trying to rub the tickly sensation away. She wouldn't come back until he'd promised not to do it again. He was still laughing as he promised.

'Anyway, I want to show you something else.'

She stood back, eyeing him, jumpy and suspicious. 'What is it?'

'Come here.'

'You promised.'

'I know. And I won't break it. Now come here.'

She was tense as a set trap as she sidled back against him and let him hold her. She flinched as he raised an arm and pointed out into the marsh.

'Come on now, trust me, I'm a salesman.'

'I'm trying.'

'Look along my arm, follow the line of my finger.'

'Mm.'

'To the edge of that wee pond, see it?'

'Oh yes, I see. What is it?'

'A great crested grebe, on its nest.'

'Really. Oh, it's lovely, isn't it?'

Shep felt her relaxing into him.

'Beautiful. And the black and white stripes by her side, see them? They're her chicks, well, their heads anyway.'

'Ducklings, really?'

'Mm, I'm not sure. Grebelings maybe?'

'Oh Shep, look at them – they're so sweet, and not ugly at all.'

'You're talking about cygnets, baby swans.'

'Well excuse me, Mister Birdwatcher. Whichever, at least they're not ugly, that's what matters.'

'Look, she's got them sheltering behind her, keeping them out of the sun.'

'Aagh.'

'See, if you come down a bit, to your left, going towards that house on its own, the brown birds, they're curlews; look at their beaks.'

'How peculiar.' Her attention rose to two birds in the air over the school, tumbling and flapping like rags in the wind. 'Look, what are they?'

'Lapwings, or peewits.'

'Which one?'

'Either, they're the same thing.'

She raised her eyebrows as she looked at him. 'How do you know all of this?'

'Curiosity, I suppose. I see so much when I'm driving, particularly up here.' He eased her off and went around to the passenger side. In the glove compartment, he moved his cigars aside and took out a book. 'I thought I'd find out.'

'*The Observer's Book of Birds*,' she said, taking the book from him. 'How funny. Big handsome Shep, the bird observer.'

'I think they're beautiful, that's all.'

'I think this is beautiful, today, this place. I could stay here forever.'

And that day, so alien and so long ago, he understood why.

Shep sat for a while, engine running, headlights piercing the gloaming across the corner of the marsh. Around its drier edge, he could see a fresh path, to a gap where the chain-link fence was pulled apart. The mark of this recent footfall was enough to give him second thoughts. Had Rebecca been right to be scared? He turned the lights off, kept the heater on full.

Fear and the need to know pulled inside his chest like two threads on either side of a knot until it became unbearable. He turned the engine off and threw open the door. The cold hit him hard. His vision swam as his eyes streamed and he stumbled in the frozen steps of last night's final gathering.

Looking back through the fence, the safety of his car felt a long way away, a different place. He'd crossed a border.

Across the marsh was an absence that was hard on the eye, a nothing that was difficult to believe. There was no evidence of the house they had moved into, the floors he had sanded, the walls he had hung with paper, the banisters and doors he had stripped of old shellac with meths and wire wool before applying Danish oil to bring out the natural grain of the timber, the porch they had sat on during those early summers, drinking beer and wine with new friends from the village until the citronella candles were no longer effective and the midges had gotten too fierce and forced them all swatting and cursing into the house, where they sat around the dining table on chairs made by John Cutter and ate snacks prepared in the kitchen he had helped Shep install.

The memory of the lost warmth of those days melted away as Shep stepped into the twilight of the trees. He recoiled, violated by the touch of frosted leaves against his face. His back ached as he bent low to creep beneath the reach of the branches. Straightening when he came to where the schoolroom used to be.

He wasn't ready for the clearing. He hesitated at its edge like a novice skater, wary of stepping onto the ice. The last time he had been here, he was alone amongst the rubble of broken walls, the smashed tiles of the collapsed roof. The air had been thick with distress. Heavy snow had continued to fall. He'd wondered at the wreckage his son had survived. Tonight it was quiet. Dark lines of footprints converged at the centre like wheel spokes. A mound provided the trampled axis that drew Shep out into the glade. He picked up the abandoned spade, recognising it as his own, and used it to move the flaps of turf apart. Steadying the blade, he put his foot across its top and pushed down.

'You don't need to do that.'

He whipped the spade out of the ground and raised it like a baseball bat, ready for all comers, searching for who had spoken.

'He's in there.'

'Who?'

'Your boy.'

There was a slight movement coming from the direction of the voice and Shep could make out a denser shadow.

'How do you know?'

A priest stepped out from the trees.

'I watched them bury him.'

'Who?'

'All of them.'

Shep returned the spade to the ground and his foot to the blade.

'I need to see.'

'He's naked. He was hit with a branch. It cracked his head. I think his neck was broken. I'd say he died instantly.'

Shep's fingers tightened around the handle.

'My name's Father Wittin.' The priest extended his hand but the offer was ignored.

'You followed me?'

'I was waiting for you.'

'You left the note?'

Wittin nodded.

'Why?'

'I thought you should know what happened.'

'So tell me.'

Wittin was just another Finnegan.

'We came to say mass. He was already here, buried up to his knees. He wasn't much more than skin and bone. He said it was his birthday. It upset people. John Cutter killed him.'

'Cutter?'

'Yes.'

'Nobody stopped him?'

'He was too quick.'

'Convenient.'

'Everybody helped bury him,' said Wittin. 'Nobody left here with clean hands or souls.'

'Including you?'

Both men stared at the ground between them.

'Would you like me to say a few words, for Dog?'

'Doug. Douglas.'

'Douglas? Douglas. I'm sorry.' The priest looked stunned. 'I didn't even know his name.'

It was the first time Shep had said his son's name in years.

'You didn't know him at all.'

'The whole village called him Dog.'

'Wasn't he part of your flock? Shouldn't you have tended him until he was back in the fold? The stray lamb, isn't that the story?'

'I failed.'

'You're a priest. Of course you failed.'

'Fuck you,' said Wittin. 'You abandoned him.'

The speed of the punch caught them both by surprise. Wittin fell backwards. Shep stood over him, hunched, fists balled, rocking and ready.

'No,' he said, 'she did. I had to leave with her.'

'Did he know that?'

Shep didn't answer. He couldn't.

His anger subsided. He slackened as Wittin got to his feet. He didn't help him.

'I shouldn't have done that.'

Wittin brushed himself down as though he hadn't heard.

'For your information, I did try to see him once, not long after I arrived. I went with the best of intentions. Sure, I wasn't going to be told by the likes of anybody in the village who I should or shouldn't be talking to. I make my own mind up. Your boy threatened me with an axe, so he did, said he'd do the same to me. He pulled his shirt up and kept pointing to the cuts across his stomach, and I thought that was what he was meaning.'

'Cuts? What do you mean? What cuts?'

'Well, more slashes I would imagine, judging by the scars,' said Wittin. 'Up here, messy, high on his stomach.'

'Who cut him?'

'I thought he'd made an attempt on his own life.'

'What?'

'It made sense all right. I'd been told he wasn't right in the head, whatever right means any more. And I thought his giving out at me was him threatening to kill me.'

'Kill you? Why?'

'Because now I think it likely that it was the priest I replaced who wounded your boy.'

'Because?'

'His remains were found in the ashes.'

'His remains?'

'Amongst others.'

'The body under the tarpaulin?'

Wittin nodded.

'He killed Finnegan?'

Wittin was surprised to hear admiration in Shep's voice.

'Good for him. Even if it wasn't self-defence, it was justified. If anybody in this village was unstable, it was that twisted fucker Finnegan. I can still hear him, his false fury, straight out of a dishonest mind.'

'What had you done to warrant this fury?'

'Accused him of fathering Mary Magnal's child.'

'Francis?'

'Francis the firstborn, as Finnegan called him, a new child, a gift from God. It was an open secret as soon as the child was seen in public. He *was* Finnegan. It was sickening, a priest corrupting things even further. I put it into words. He had the temerity to scream at me to get out. "This is my house, a house of God," he said. "Get out, get out, get out." He doused me with holy water. "Why don't you burn? Why don't you burn? Why?" and "Why didn't he die with her?" That's when I realised.'

Wittin dragged his open-palmed hands down his face before speaking over his fingertips. 'Mary's first child was his?'

Shep nodded.

'You couldn't make it up. Lucy Magnal wasn't the result of a one-night stand at the dancing in the city, for which Mary was forever repenting, always in the church. He'd lost his daughter.'

'A daughter he had no right to.'

'None.'

'The first grave on the right when you leave the church.'

'He attacked me by persecuting my wife. I beat him. Last time I saw Finnegan, he was on the floor, nose and spirit broken.'

'And he took it out on your son.'

'Well, he tried.'

Clouds pulled away from the moon and they saw each other clearly as the first flake of snow fell between them and landed on the grave. It melted and was replaced at once by another, and another. Both men looked away. The flakes were dense and thick, like ghost ash from a distant pyre, whispering through the leaves, where they lodged, collected and rendered the trees Christmassy. Sound was brought to ground. Neither man spoke as the snowfall cleansed and calmed.

The snow stuck and formed a layer over the flattened ground of the murder. It would have been easy to believe that nothing had happened, had the snow not continued to melt on the mound that covered the body, forming a niveous iris around a sharp black pupil.

'Listen, you're probably not all the same,' said Shep. 'Nonetheless, I don't have any need. Why don't you go?'

Wittin left.

Shep knelt.

The cold and the wet soaked into his trousers. He bent to be closer to Douglas. The image of his son's twisted body filled his head. He was scared and shaking as his fingers dug into the ground. His lips parted to say he was sorry.

# 23

Rebecca looked out of the window for the umpteenth time. There was still a space where their car used to be, matt against the glittering frost on the rest of the road. She closed the curtains, fixing them so that they hung straight, and walked the floor, agitated. She pulled open the drawer on the bedside cabinet. It was empty. So was its companion on the other side of the bed, as well as the drawers in the dresser and the desk. She rifled through the spare bedding in the wardrobe and scoured each of the shelves, behind the iron and the hairdryer, room-service menus and laundry bags.

Downstairs, she hit the reception bell harder than she had intended and jumped at the sound it produced. She jumped again as the door behind the counter opened and Glen Masson rushed out.

'What's the matter; is everything okay?'

'Yes – yes, I'm sorry. I didn't mean to hit it so hard. I'm so sorry, it was silly of me.'

'Please, that's okay,' he said, raising his hand to calm Rebecca, dismissing her apologies and making time to gather himself. 'Goodness, you had me going.' His concern was replaced by his natural desire to be of help as he came around the counter. 'I'm glad it's nothing serious, that's all. I think maybe that's the loudest the bell's ever been rung.'

'I'm so—'

'You tested it,' he said. 'At least we know it works under pressure.'

'You're very understanding.'

'Nonsense. Now, what can I do for you?'

'Well, you see, Shep, my husband, he's been away for quite a while now and I was getting concerned and I didn't really know what to do with myself and so I was looking for a bible, so I could read or maybe pray, because praying always calms me, and I—'

'You couldn't find a bible?'

'Yes.'

'There isn't one, I'm afraid.'

Rebecca was flummoxed.

'But I thought you had to …'

'No.'

'But what about the Gideons, don't they still give them to hotels?'

'Possibly, but they haven't made it this far yet. There's a church just across the street. You could pray there, if you wrap up warm. I don't think it's ever locked.'

'I don't know. What if Shep comes back?'

'You could leave a note,' said Glen, 'or I could listen out for him, if you'd like, let him know where you are. Whatever, I don't mind.'

Rebecca was struck by Glen Masson's genuine manner, his untroubled stare and the soft, blemish-free complexion.

'I'll think about it. Thank you for your help.'

'You're welcome,' he said. 'It's why we're here. Just ring if you need us.' He pinged the desk bell on his way back around the counter. 'And I'll be sure to get bibles, for those who need them. I have to admit, it never crossed my mind.'

Smiling, yet liking him a little less for this comment, Rebecca went back upstairs.

Crossing the room, she opened the curtains again and looked up the street. She was challenged by the fact that the lights of the church were on and that even after all she had been subjected to within those walls, its call remained. She drew and restraightened the curtains. The church lights remained visible through their fabric.

A few minutes later, wearing a scarf, hat and gloves, she put a note on the bed and left the door unlocked. Toggling her duffle as she strode down the corridor, she turned left out of the hotel and walked up the street towards the church, with purpose at first, but losing confidence with each step that took her closer.

She had forgotten that they lay together. She stood paralysed as the steeple towered over her. Fresh flowers had been placed on every grave that lined the path, some in matching vases, others in pots; simple bouquets laid on the ground or showy presentations bound with ribbon in individual plastic reservoirs that had turned to ice. They were another way of excluding her. She knew what had been at the back of Finnegan's mind when his impassioned bleating had cajoled a grieving community into the collective burial. He wanted her to know that she wasn't one of them, didn't belong to his congregation. She had never been thankful that her son was not one of the names on the headstones that stood out as crisp as the day they were carved.

Rebecca's walk to the church door was like passing through a revenant playground. Each name evoked the sound and spirit of the child interred, and she could hear them. Their fear and confusion and innocent questioning of what had happened and why not everybody was there, the class being incomplete.

She stepped inside. It was warmer than she could remember it ever being, enhancing the incense, wood polish and candle smoke; smells familiar to most churches, here entwined into a blend as singular and distinct to this village church as malt whisky was to its distillery. Stopping at her old pew, she put her handbag down and genuflected. But something stopped her taking her place. She wanted to sit, to kneel and pray. She couldn't. The succour she sought wasn't there. She was swamped by the vicious memories of Finnegan's rage. A rage that had poured from him undiluted until the day she could take no more and had walked that aisle for what she believed would be the last time. Beaten by the past, Rebecca picked up her handbag and turned to leave.

'Don't go.'

She caught the scream in her throat. She clamped her lapels closed around her neck with one hand and held onto the pew for support with the other. The voice echoed until there was dead silence.

'It's me. Over here.'

Deborah moved out of the transept into the nave, briefly backlit as she passed in front of the burning candles, so that Rebecca could see her.

'Deborah?'

'Hello, Becky.'

They met at the front pew.

'You look nice,' said Deborah.

'Thank you.'

'I never thought I'd see you again.'

Rebecca looked uncomfortable under Deborah's scrutiny. Deborah took hold of her and hugged her.

'How did you find out so quickly?'

They both knew what they were talking about.

'John called, early yesterday morning.'

'That surprises me, I must say.'

'His duty, I suppose.'

'Just arrived?'

'No. We made the journey yesterday, arrived late last night.'

'You've seen the house?'

Rebecca pointed. 'You were lighting candles. I hope I didn't interrupt your prayers?'

'No,' said Deborah. 'No. I was just lighting candles.'

The flames danced in Rebecca's eyes.

'Don't count them, please.' Deborah moved to obscure the candles from her view and Rebecca believed she knew how many there were.

'Will you sit with me?' Rebecca asked.

'Why?'

'Company mostly. Is that okay?'

'That sounds nice.'

They sat on the front pew. Rebecca loosened her coat and laid her bag beside her.

'How have you been?' she said.

'Off the rails mostly.' The look Deborah gave her left Rebecca in no doubt that this was the truth. 'You?'

'Unhappy; trying not to be, for Shep mostly.'

'He still blames himself?'

'Hates himself. Always will.'

'I never understood why. None of it was his fault.'

Rebecca didn't answer. They sat for a while. She was conscious of Deborah's attention.

'You're still so beautiful, you know that? I so wish I had your looks.'

'You do. You just don't have a Shep, the peace of mind that brings. He could have walked away from us both. Maybe that would have been best, all three of us going our separate ways.'

'What have you been doing with yourself?'

'I'm not fit for much really. I try and look after Shep. I pray every day. We live opposite a church. It's not as nice as this, but I feel safe there, unjudged.'

'What do you pray for?'

'For what happened the other night. Now I'll be praying for forgiveness.'

'You've got nothing to ask forgiveness for, Becky.'

'You never did judge people. I liked that about you.'

'How's your eye? You're not wearing your patch.'

Rebecca slid her wedding ring off her finger as Deborah traced the scar. Raising the ring to her eye, she tapped against glass.

'It sees no evil.'

She smiled as Deborah withdrew.

'It would be my party piece.'

'Shit, Becky, I'm so sorry. And you think you need forgiveness?'

'What I prayed for was more than an eye for an eye.'

'You got your wish. He must be listening.'

Rebecca took Deborah's hand. 'It wasn't a wish, Debbie, it was a prayer, and he's always listening.'

'Why do you think he waited so long?'

'That's for him to know.'

'Well you deserved the answer; we all did.'

Deborah slid her fingers between Rebecca's, rough against their stony smooth. Rebecca stroked Deborah's knuckles, still open and red from the burning night's activity.

'Debbie, do you feel any better?'

'I feel relieved. I sense a future.'

'Does that make you feel bad?'

'Not in the slightest.'

'Me neither. But it doesn't make me feel good.'

'Feeling good; remember that?'

Deborah's gaze was drawn to the blues of the stained-glass window, the rippling seas at the foot of the cross, fishermen hauling loaded nets of glinting fish, so many they were close to being swamped, killed by their bounty.

'He made wishes,' said Deborah. 'Douglas, I mean.'

Deborah felt Rebecca's fingers tense around hers.

'You wouldn't be spiteful?'

'No, I wouldn't. I'd rather not have found out.'

'What kind of wishes?'

'Silver ones, shaped like boats, made out of sweetie tinfoil. They were all together, in a dip between the roots of my Jenny's tree. Freaked us out at first, knowing he'd been there.'

'Us?'

Deborah looked away. She tried to take her hand

back, but Rebecca held it, her grip firm and supportive. Deborah relaxed, grateful she hadn't been released. She stared at the floor, rearranged the dust with her feet.

'Sabbath,' she said quietly, into her chest, as if trying to keep it to herself. 'I went with Sabbath.'

'I don't know her.'

'You wouldn't.' Deborah's voice shrank to a whisper. 'She was a wise little girl who understood; listened.'

'Was?'

Deborah nodded. 'She's gone.' She let Rebecca place an arm around her, bring her close. 'We all need somebody, Becky. I was alone.'

'You sound embarrassed. You shouldn't be.'

Deborah sniffed as she smiled at Rebecca.

'I'm not. She helped.' She took a breath to steady herself. Sitting back, she released it in weary expiration. Rebecca took her arm from around her as her breathing steadied. 'I didn't realise she would go so soon, when I found his wishes at Jenny's tree. I got used to her being at my side. But she wasn't. And she didn't come when I called. I knew she was gone.'

'You don't need her any more.'

'I know. But I liked her.'

Rebecca slipped her wedding ring back on.

'Jenny's tree. He liked Jenny, I remember that.'

'Really?'

'He said she was nice to him, used to leave him sweets, in his desk. He liked sweets as well. What little boy doesn't?' She shared an uncertain smile with Deborah, who responded with one of her own and almost instantly tried to hide it when Rebecca continued. 'Or little girl?

She was the only one he talked about.'

'That feels weird, sorry.'

'It shouldn't. We spent a lot of time together, when he was younger. Even when other people stopped coming to visit, you came, with Jenny and John, for much longer.'

'He changed.'

'I know. He was never easy. I didn't blame people.'

'He got worse.'

'Much worse.'

'What he did to you.'

'What he did to Alice.'

'To them all,' said Deborah.

'I saw that, of all people, the cursed creator. He was my fault. It was my fault. Why do you think I pray?'

'No. Nobody thinks that, about you or Shep.'

Rebecca held Deborah's hand tightly for a moment before letting it go. Her good eye showed she didn't believe Deborah. There was compassion in it as she turned Deborah's face to hers.

'It's okay to blame me. I brought him into the world. Everybody else is without sin.'

'Did you ever love him?'

Deborah waited. Unable to read her, she took Rebecca's silence to be a no.

'In a way, I envy you. It must be easier not to have those feelings hooked into your heart, straining your flesh.'

'Why would you say that? Don't you think I know I should have? It makes what I did worse, Deborah. You hated him for surviving. I should have loved him for the same reason, rejoiced, not been tormented.'

Deborah didn't know how to respond. The strangeness of the exchange made her falter. She didn't want Rebecca to suffer any more because of what she might say.

'Anyway,' said Deborah, 'he made wishes.'

'You know what he was wishing for, don't you? The girl who liked him: the one who was nice to him at school.'

'The "one" who was nice. God, that sounds so pathetic.'

'Deborah, don't blaspheme.'

'I find it hard to do anything else in this place. Surprised you're here at all, the way you were treated.'

'One priest can't be used to blame a whole church.'

'Where we live, here, so small and so far from everywhere else, they *are* the church.'

Rebecca didn't try to contradict her.

'Strange,' Deborah said, 'being here together again.'

'It is. As you said, it's a long time since I was welcome.'

'Feels strange being here at all.'

'Seven years,' said Rebecca.

'I can't remember most of it, not the details anyway. Only the way I've felt; which is what I wanted to forget.'

'Praying for his death kept me going; was my purpose. He was thirteen the day he survived; twenty the day he died.'

'We knew,' said Deborah.

Rebecca turned to her, curious as to what she meant.

'"It's my birthday" – his last words. As if we needed reminding.'

'How would you know?'

'Know what?'

'His last words. If he died in a fire.'

Deborah couldn't retract what she'd said. She couldn't avoid Rebecca's question.

'Shep was right, wasn't he? He knew straight away.'

'It was at the school. It wasn't planned. We didn't know he'd be there.'

'Deborah,' said Rebecca, suddenly anxious, 'is he really gone?'

'He's gone.'

'You're certain?'

'I saw it. We all did. We all buried him.'

Rebecca's face softened with relief.

'So Shep's safe?'

'Why wouldn't he be?'

'He went to the school. Someone left a note.'

Deborah considered the otherwise empty church and knew who'd left the note; the only one who felt guilty.

'He's safe.'

'I told him not to go. He wouldn't listen. Shep knew best, as usual. He'll come back, and we can go home, because he's gone.'

Rebecca's smile was joyous, as infectious as it was improper.

'Good for you,' said Deborah.

'It's only the second prayer he's ever answered.'

'And the first was?'

'Conception.'

Deborah burst out laughing. Rebecca watched, perplexed.

'Jesus, Becky, I'd say answering the second was the least he could do.'

Rebecca let the blasphemy slide but looked a little

hurt at Deborah's laughter even as it subsided. They both faced her Jesus in the stained-glass window.

'What was it he said, at the end?' asked Deborah.

'"Forgive them, Father, for they know not what they do."'

'You think that applies to us all?'

'I pray so.'

'Me too.'

Deborah stood and fastened her jacket.

'Leaving?'

'Yes. I don't belong here, don't like what it does to people.'

'But you lit candles for the children.'

'And their teacher. Like I said, they're just candles, not a moment of weakness.'

'We all need somebody, you also said that.'

'I need John.' Deborah pulled her collar up. 'It's nice to see you, Becky, despite it all.'

She kissed Rebecca on the cheek.

'You staying?'

'Yes. I'll wait for Shep. He'll know.'

Rebecca listened to Deborah's footsteps receding. She waited for the door to open and close before she sank to the kneeler and bowed her head to pray.

'Thank you,' she said, before she was overcome and her body was convulsed with sobbing.

Douglas 'Dog' Evans, 13

*Seven years earlier*

Dog Evans had bark and bite. He was never called Dog to his face. From his window seat at the back of the room he would often growl like a hungry beast as though in two minds as to which back to pounce on, which neck to sink his teeth into. Heads would stay bent over work and nobody would turn around.

He was a known user of knives and a master of their concealment. When instructed to open his satchel, lift his desk lid or turn out his pockets, he was always unarmed. Moments later, the teacher satisfied, a blade would flash in his hand for the benefit of one of his classmates. He would watch this news spread amongst them and purr.

In Douglas's early school years, at the start of his gradual estrangement, the mere glint of a knife had caused Calvin Struan to urinate himself in the playground. The following day, in terror of it happening again, he gave Douglas his chocolate bar. Douglas was unaware that a precedent had been set. He never visited the tuck shop again.

A cordon of space and silence grew around him. Nobody strayed too close or said anything too loud. They simply bowed their heads to escape.

Jonny Raffique was the only one with any steel. Douglas

thought to challenge him. But Jonny had the voice of an outlaw and eyes that were wholly black, conferring upon him the possibility of unknown strength and untapped skills and therefore the potential for defeat. Douglas tried to ignore him.

It got so he couldn't ignore Alice Corggie. Each signal she gave to Raffique was noticed by Douglas. He followed her, cornered her and touched her. He put his hand where he thought she wanted Jonny Raffique's to be. He took it away when she opened her mouth to scream, placing it over her lips, sealing her until she was sucking against his palm, and he felt her tears and saw her fear.

Dr Corggie and his wife complained. The school board sent a representative to speak to Douglas and his mortified parents. The nature of the assault led to two weeks' exclusion. When Father Finnegan came and lectured him about sin and the evils committed by the hand, Dog Evans refused to blink and the priest couldn't match his stare. Teacher and parents alike thought it best to shroud the enforced absence with an unspecified illness, to protect Alice's dignity. For two weeks, Dog Evans stared out of his window across the marsh to the school, thinking about Alice Corggie, masturbating relentlessly. Rebecca couldn't bring herself to wash his bed linen. She dragged it from his bed by a corner and left it in a pile for Shep to pick up. She gave her son clean linen and told him to make his own bed. It was the last time she entered his room.

On the day of his return to school, Shep used the worsening conditions as a reason to stay in the village, confining himself to doing what business he could on the telephone or catching up with paperwork. Rebecca stayed in bed. Shep cooked breakfast. Douglas prowled around with his coat on, swinging his bag, impatient, growling, caged. Shep put sausage, bacon, tea and toast on the table.

'Sit down and eat something.'

'I'm not hungry.'

'You need to eat something'

'I don't. I want to go.'

'It's early, look at the snow, it'll be cold.'

'I won't feel it.'

Douglas touched objects and examined things he was indifferent to, just to be moving.

'You need money?'

'No.'

'Okay, go on then.'

Douglas went to the door.

'Stay away from Alice Corggie,' said Shep.

Shep was sure he caught an insolent leer, but Douglas was gone before he had the chance to repeat the warning.

Despite leaving early and skipping over his well-worn route across the marshland, safe and dry, Dog Evans wasn't the first to arrive at school. He was surprised to see the older children all there, gathered around Jonny Raffique. He studied them as he stepped from the marsh and walked through the gate. Calvin Struan hid behind the Longfields and showed no sign of coming forward with his offering for protection. It was the first time this had happened since Dog had caused Calvin to soil himself. Alice Corggie stood at Raffique's side.

He heard the sound and saw the light from Mr Corrigan's car as it approached the school, wheels spinning in the slushy troughs of the lane. As he slid into his parking space, wet tyres bumping against a tree trunk set horizontal in the ground for this purpose, Dog Evans' shadow raced across the playground and engulfed the children. The lights died. The car door opened. Mr Corrigan climbed out and slammed it shut.

'Good morning, Douglas, good to have you back,' he said with hollow enthusiasm. 'I hope you're recovered. Ready to work?'

Dog Evans ignored him.

Mr Corrigan noticed the other children as he passed Douglas and crossed the yard. He also noticed the fact that none of them smiled or said hello to the boy.

'Quite a welcome, Douglas, you must have been missed.' He pulled a face to the contrary for the benefit of the class. Calvin Struan snorted, forcing snot from his nose. The other children made a wild play over Calvin's hanging bogey and the tension broke as they all jeered at him leaning forward so it didn't swing onto his mackintosh while he fumbled for his handkerchief. Only Jonny Raffique and Alice Corggie kept their attention fixed on Dog Evans, watching for his response. He was glaring at Mr Corrigan's back as the teacher skipped up the three steps to the door to the school. As he took his keys from his pocket, Mr Corrigan turned with a half-smirk still on his face. He saw Dog Evans. The smirk disappeared. His hands out in contrition, he took a step back down to the yard.

'Come on now, Douglas, just a wee joke, trying to

lighten things a bit for your first day back. We're laughing with you, not at—'

He never finished his sentence. His mouth went useless and he covered his ears as Dog Evans split the morning with a scream that was all animal and wrath. Bulging eyes. Reddening skin that tightened and pulled every muscle in his neck into fibrous relief. It lasted many seconds. Although directed at the teacher, the scream had a devastating effect on the children. Most turned away, protecting their ears, some losing their footing as they tried to get out of range. The Longfields, immune to the squealing of stuck pigs, gaped in awe as they took backwards steps. Jenny Cutter forced hair into her mouth in panic and scratched at her thigh. Jonny Raffique was unnerved yet held Alice Corggie as she pulled tight against him, her face buried in his shoulder. Kerr Munson dropped his pen. Calvin Struan urinated. Lucy Magnal gripped her wooden cross. Muchis choked on a cola chew. Maggie Voar tried to go to Mr Corrigan, who had slipped on the step and fallen, but was pulled back by Robbie and Cameron, wailing for her to stay. Some began to cry. When Dog Evans stopped, the sniffling filled the air.

He shifted his attention from the teacher as he sucked draughts of air through his mouth, wet with saliva. His chest heaved as he inspected each of his classmates while his breathing stabilised. The only movement was the avoidance of his stare, the chewing of a lip. Dog Evans swallowed as though hungry. Satisfied, he looked back to the teacher and said, 'Ring the bell.'

Mr Corrigan stood up and brushed himself down. He

addressed Dog Evans with as much control as he could muster.

'You're not coming back into my classroom.'

Dog Evans took slow, deliberate steps towards the shaking teacher, not once breaking eye contact.

'I'm going into my room.'

Mr Corrigan backed up to the school door, unlocked it and pushed it open.

'Now, before I let anybody else in.'

The children shrank away as Dog Evans turned his gaze on them, gathering beneath the lamp in the protective aura of Jonny Raffique. Dog Evans searched for a sign of weakness. Snowfall obscured Raffique and his dependants and a false peace descended. Dog Evans allowed himself to blink.

'It's my birthday tomorrow,' he said. 'Don't forget.'

Mr Corrigan moved out of his way as Dog Evans climbed the steps and entered the school. From within the boy's chest gurgled something akin to laughter, a further mockery.

Dog Evans could hear Mr Corrigan following him as he walked down the side of the classroom, opened the storeroom, went inside and slumped down into the corner. He closed the door to the sound of the teacher's retreat.

A muffled dispute followed. The only voices he could make out were Alice Corrgie's, strident and demanding, and the squeaky whining of those happy little bastards, the Voars.

Mr Corrigan re-entered the classroom alone, his footsteps irresolute, creeping almost. They stopped outside the storeroom. His breathing was heavy and it was obvious when he held it. The key was in and turned in an instant.

'I'm sorry, Douglas,' he said. 'You scared the little ones. I'll let you out for lunch.'

'I won't be hungry.'

'You'll need the toilet, at least.'

Dog Evans stood up and pulled his zip down.

'I won't.'

He knew the teacher could hear him pissing in the dark as the key shifted in the lock, but Mr Corrigan didn't turn it.

'Shit. Douglas, stop that, now.'

'Can't.'

'Why are you doing this?'

'Because you locked me in here.'

The room boomed as the teacher kicked the door.

'Well you can fucking lie in it, you hear? I've had enough. You'll get out when I say so.'

'Finished.'

Mr Corrigan stormed away and could be heard ordering the rest of the class into the room. There was no conversation to speak of. Boots stomped through the class to the back where coats were taken off and hung up on hooks with names below and gym kits waiting in gym bags. Chairs scraped and desk lids clapped.

'Sir,' said Connor, 'will he …'

'No, it's okay, Connor. He's locked in, he can't get out.'

'Like a jail?'

'No, not like a jail.'

'Like a zoo,' said Jonny Raffique, prompting sniggers

that caused Dog Evans to stand and press his face against the ventilation holes drilled in the door. Dog Evans watched.

'No, Jonny, not like a zoo either. And I don't think that's a nice way to talk about somebody, anybody.'

'A dog, though?'

'That's enough.'

Jonny let it go.

'Like an asylum,' said Jack Todd, deadpan.

Mr Corrigan frowned at Jack. The class fell quiet, waiting for the teacher to respond, to challenge Jack or tell him off. He didn't.

Mad Dog listened.

'Okay, books out, everybody. We'll start with arithmetic. If anybody needs a sharp pencil, put your hand up and Alice will bring you one.'

Alice Corggie looked over and quickly turned away.

'Sir.'

'Alice?'

Her raised arm directed the teacher and the rest of the class to the storeroom. Mr Corrigan sagged and leant on his desk, shielding his eyes with his right hand. His left formed a hard white fist around his fountain pen. Dog Evans could see his lips moving. He assumed the teacher was praying, like his mother did. He knew it wouldn't do him or his charges any good. His mother's prayers had never been answered; he'd heard them, he was still here. Mr Corrigan's lips stopped moving. He raised his head and his eyes came out from behind his hand, making direct contact with Dog Evans. He stood. His chair fell backwards into the blackboard.

Kerr Munson checked his watch. It was seven minutes and thirty-seven seconds past nine when Mr Corrigan unlocked the storeroom door. Kerr noted this in his journal. Dog Evans had the circular impressions of the ventilation holes across the left side of his face where he had been pressed against the door watching Alice Corggie. He was erect, aching with what he wanted to do to her.

'Go home.'

Dog Evans took his ache back across the marsh.

He charged up the path to the door in the opposite direction to Shep's new tracks.

Inside, the fire was roaring and Rebecca was at the table drinking tea. She jumped up, startled and uneasy as he burst into the house.

'Why are you here?'

As if the question referred to his very existence, Dog Evans swung his school satchel at his mother. The buckle slashed her eye. Rebecca spun backwards, knocking the breakfast things from the table as she fell. Blood seeped between her fingers as Dog Evans stood over her.

'Because you wanted me. I am your dog, bitch.'

When Shep came back from the post office, he saw his son's returning tracks and noticed the front door was open. Wiping his feet, he went inside. Things were out of place, beyond untidy. He listened, uneasy, for any glitch in the silence.

'Rebecca. Rebecca.'

'Shep.'

Seeing the blood on the floor at the same time as he heard the slip of the bathroom lock, Shep took the stairs two at a time.

'Rebecca?'

She stood on the landing. The stains on the cotton towel ran from pink to crimson. It concealed half of her face. Blood was drying on the back of her hand, down her arm and on the front of her jumper.

'Jesus, Becky.'

She fought his need to pull the towel away, but he insisted. He couldn't hide his shock. Her skin was torn; a slash, ripping from the corner of her eye across the lid, that would need stitches.

'Can you see?'

'I don't know.'

'Rebecca, what happened?'

'He came home.'

Her free hand pointed to his bedroom. Shep kicked the door with all he had and followed it into the room, slapping and punching his son the moment he was within reach. The boy cowered and guarded his head from the initial onslaught before pushing back and asserting himself, hefting Shep away with surprising force.

'Rebecca, Rebecca, Rebecca, Rebecca, Rebecca. Always her.'

Shep's anger continued in another wave of fists. When it subsided, his chest heaved in rhythm with his panting. His son lowered his arms and stood to his full insolent height.

'Finished?'

Shep knew he'd broken something between them.

'Stop, Shep, please.' Rebecca stood in the doorway. 'Please, leave him, come away.'

'Leave me. Go away. Typical.'

'Look what you've done to your mother, what do you expect?'

'Some mothering.'

Rebecca gasped. Shep heard her running down the stairs.

'You're in trouble,' said Shep, a threatening finger inches from his son's face. 'Don't go anywhere until I get back, and so help me God, you'd better pray she's okay.'

He ran from the room in pursuit of Rebecca.

Dog Evans stood motionless, listening to the car sheering in the snow as the over-revved wheels spun until they hit gravel and Shep swerved away from the house.

Holding his curtain aside, he saw the car's tail lights as they veered onto Main Street.

'I don't pray,' he said, shifting his attention to the school and thoughts of Alice Corggie.

Blinded by the snow and the morning still black with night, Dog Evans picked his way across the marsh, hat pulled over his ears and a scarf-concealed face.

Avoiding the main gate, he skirted the school grounds until he knew he would be out of sight of the village. Turning on his small torch, he approached the rear wall where the friendship bench sat below Hamilton Walker's window. Taking his hunting knife from his pocket, he slid it between the sash windows, slicing through the draught excluder before turning the blade around to use the spine to force the fastener open. The weights dropped in the pulley void as the bottom window slid up.

Pushing off the top of the bench took Dog Evans

through the space in one swift movement, dragging snow from the sill over Hamilton Walker's desk. Once inside, he shut the window against the outside and closed the fastener.

The teacher's key was in the top drawer of his desk, a steel mortise on a green fob. Dog Evans took it, walked between the desks and unlocked the storeroom. He inserted the key into the lock on the inside. The wall clock above the coat rack on the back wall showed just after six when he opened the first Bunsen burner. There was a gentle sigh of gas. Walking the length of the workbench, he opened all twelve, six pairs. Corner to corner, he worked his way around the class, turning the four ceiling-mounted gas heaters fully on. Satisfied with the sibilant hiss of escaping gas, he sat in Alice Corggie's seat.

Lifting the lid, he bent to examine the contents of her desk: exercise books covered with harpooned hearts and Raffique's initials, pencils, a geometry set in a tin case, Wrigley's, perfume, cherry lip balm, a small purse containing two sanitary pads, a photograph of Raffique on the Golden Gate Bridge, and a woollen scarf.

Holding the scarf to his face, Dog Evans chewed gum as he defaced her books. Turning the photograph into confetti, he tossed it into the air, declaring Alice Corggie and himself man and wife, spitting saliva and gum all over Raffique's desktop. He sniffed as the pieces fell. The smell was strengthening. Taking her perfume, he retreated to the storeroom, locking himself in. Jamming Alice's scarf into the gap at the base of the door and taping over the ventilation holes sealed him in. Emptying the bottle of perfume over the stench of yesterday's piss, he settled into the corner, unzipped, wanked, wiped, rezipped and fell asleep.

# 24

Although Wittin didn't recognise the woman who faced him down the aisle, a taper in her hand, two rows of candles in front of her, he knew who she was before the door closed behind him. She paid him no attention until he stood beside her.

'One for each child?' he asked.

'And their teacher, Mr Corrigan; each with an apology.'

'They're dead. Who are you apologising to?'

'I'm apologising *from*.'

'You remember their names?'

'And what they looked like, how they laughed and screamed, who cried and who fought, who was pretty, who was handsome, who waved from a horse; how all of their parents looked at me in the days after they died.'

'I pity you.'

'You should.'

Wittin examined Rebecca's face in the candlelight.

'What?'

'You don't look how I expected.'

'You thought the dog's bitch would be ugly?'

'That's ugly language and it's not what I meant.'

She held him with her eye until he conceded.

'You're right,' he said, 'it is what I meant. I'm sorry.'

Rebecca blinked, turned away, lit the last candle.

'You don't look much like a priest.'

'How do you know I am one?'

'You look lost, and the worse for wear. This place affects us all.'

Wittin considered his condition, collarless and blood-stained.

'Well, you've your husband to blame for the blood.'

'Really?' Rebecca couldn't stop herself from smiling. 'My Shep did that to you?'

'I'm impressed you find his actions and my situation amusing, bearing in mind the events that have passed.'

'He has a thing for priests. You're the second one he's hit to my knowledge. You must have upset him.'

'I accused him of abandoning his son.'

Rebecca extinguished the taper between her finger and thumb. She put it back and made the sign of the cross in front of the candles. He saw her lips move in silent prayer. Then they spoke to him.

'I would have hit you,' she said, blunt and unequivocal. 'You deserved it. Although you spoke from a position of ignorance, that is no excuse for passing poor judgement upon a good man. You assumed too much whilst know-ing too little.'

'But he did abandon him. He left him.'

'He didn't leave me. I needed him. Our son neither wanted nor needed either of us. Shep wanted him.'

Wittin took a few steps back from her certainty; tired, impatient, irritated, and yes, she was right, lost.

'So it was okay,' he said, 'to leave him? I mean – that passed as right, leave a child to fend for himself?'

'Shep didn't. He wasn't. You don't understand.'

She was so sure of what she was saying it destabilised him and he knew he was struggling.

'Seriously, don't give me the you-don't-have-children speech, let alone dead children; because I'm so fucking beyond it I couldn't tell you. This place is all-consuming misery.'

'What do you expect?'

Rebecca was being serious. She wanted to know. Wittin approached her.

'Some celebration, about what they were, when they were here, the good years they had. For everybody's sake, in some small way, bring them back and make their lives important. Christ rose from his grave to give meaning.'

'When he was allowed to.'

'What?'

'When he was seen to have risen.'

'What?'

'The stone wasn't rolled aside to let Jesus out, it was to let witnesses in. The women had to see it, the empty chamber, to believe he had risen. To believe the miracle the resurrection had to be witnessed.'

'You've snapped,' he said. 'In here.'

He jabbed at Rebecca's temple. She continued to make it clear for him, calm and convinced.

'They had to see him in his grave. Now they can celebrate what could have been.'

'Are you insane, woman? They killed your son.'

'They had to.'

Speechless, Wittin had to walk away. Rebecca crossed herself and apologised to the candles once more before following him. He stood at the foot of the altar steps, arms hanging loose at his sides, staring at the window as if he had no idea who it was or what it was supposed to mean. He liked the colours. Rebecca ascended the steps and stood in front of him, filling his vision. She looked down upon him and spoke.

'I needn't seek the shelter of insanity, Father. I have the shelter of my faith. You do have souls to tend, however few. You should wash and dress to attend them. They will need you. When you feel you're ready, I'd like you to hear my confession.'

He almost laughed at the suggestion, quickly dismissing the idea as ridiculous to the point of blasphemy. She remained straight-faced, waiting for his answer. He was compelled to be honest.

'I don't feel worthy or capable any more,' he said. 'I'm humbled by the strength of your faith. How can you?'

'Without my faith, where would I be?'

'Where I am.'

Rebecca stepped down and stood together with Wittin, facing the same way.

'Looking up at him,' she said.

She left him at the altar. He followed her progress along the gospel walkway to the confessional. Watching her step inside, he felt his cheeks warming. He looked up at the window and saw sacrifice in death and began to understand. Rubbing the stubble on his chin and noticing the cold skin of his exposed neck, he genuflected, crossed himself and headed to the vestry.

'I want to see her room again. I need to.'

John Cutter was caught off guard by the question and

her appearance. It was the Deborah Cutter he remembered.

'You can't stop me, John, it's our house.'

'I know, I built it for you.'

Years of emptiness hit him like a branch across the back of the head. He felt a sudden weakness in his legs. His fist tightened around the door handle she had chosen.

'Please, come in.'

Deborah's hand brushed John's arm as she entered her home. He didn't pull away. She took in the disarray of the counter, the full sink, the bough on the mantelpiece, the whisky bottle and glass next to the single bed, pushed against the wall. She crossed to the bed and turned back to John.

'How long?'

'Since you left.'

'Why?'

'Not really something I could put into words Debs.'

She smiled at the abbreviated form of her name and the tacit admittance of violence in the place of those words.

'Something you put into actions?'

'I'm not proud.'

'You were never a violent man.'

'You know that's not true.'

'Not to people.'

'It's always been in me. You saw it, two nights ago.'

'You never hurt me.'

'I scared you. I scared Jenny.'

Deborah didn't deny it.

'What were you scared of?' she asked.

'Everything I couldn't prevent.'

John Cutter broke eye contact, walked to the stairwell and pulled the drape aside. Deborah followed.

'The light works,' he said. 'I changed the bulb.'

Deborah looked up into the gloom. 'You were up there?'

'Had to talk to somebody, after what I did.'

'Why not me? I was there, you saw me. I know you did.'

'I wanted her to know he was gone; it was me killed him.'

'Why?'

'I made her a promise. It was important she knew I'd kept it.'

Pulling on the light cord, Deborah lit up the landing and the two bedroom doors. She saw the brackets.

'Our lovely door, John, all your work.'

'My doing – worse behind it. I didn't want to go back in, even by accident, or if I was drunk.'

'Or missed me?'

'I determined not to.'

'And you have been determined.'

John either ignored her last comment or had no response. He pointed upstairs.

'You want some privacy? I'm happy to stay down here. In case you want to say something private.'

'About you?'

'About anything. Now that it's over.'

Deborah appeared to be scrutinising the landing but he could tell there was something else on her mind.

'What is it?' he said.

'I met Becky. In the church. She lost her eye.'

'I'm sorry to hear that. I didn't notice.'

'She's still pretty, though. She got a new one, it's glass.' Deborah hesitated. 'She's glad he's dead, John.'

'Who isn't?'

She twisted the ends of her hair between her fingers. 'Shep, maybe. Becky said Shep's at the school.'

'Why? How would he know?'

'I don't know how, or who, but he went there.'

John Cutter became agitated. 'Shit, Deborah, why didn't you tell me this straight away?'

'I don't know.'

He strode to the fire and took the bloodied bough from the mantelpiece.

'Where are you going with that?'

'The school, where else?'

'You're not going to hurt Shep?'

'I don't intend to, no.'

'What then? Why go?'

'If he's at the school, he knows that what I told him today was untrue.' John Cutter took his coat off the radiator. He took his cuffs from his police belt. There was a clink as they hit the gold in his pocket. 'I'm going to be honest with the man. We were friends.'

'What's going to happen to you, to us all?'

'I couldn't say any more. Everything's changed.'

He gave the club to Deborah to hold as he buttoned up.

'I have to ask you a question. Was it you that set fire to the house?'

'Why?'

'Deborah.'

'So what if it was? Does anybody care?'

'Have you told anybody it was you, in as many words?'

'No, why?'

'Don't. And deny it if anyone says it was. You saw the Evans' house burning and you went to watch. Give me time to try and get a story out.'

She handed the club back to him.

'I don't understand.'

'There was someone inside.'

'Please, John. That isn't funny.'

'I know.'

Deborah blanched. She wound her fingers tight through her hair, pulling it straight, pushing a blonde twist between her teeth. She chewed on it, shaking her head.

'It was Nugget.'

She shuddered and started to fall. John caught her, thinking she was going to a full faint. He held her. She was unsteady. Beads of sweat formed on her nose just below the line of freckles she hated and he thought was the prettiest thing about her face.

'No,' she said, 'I don't believe you. He can't have been. Why would anybody be in there, what reason? It's ridiculous.' She shrugged herself out of his grip and away from him. 'What are you doing, saying something like that? I thought you were being nice.'

'There was money, lots from what I'm told. He wanted to get it before anybody else found it. You know what he was like with money.'

'The money,' she said. 'Little boats.'

'Little boats?'

'All over the floor. But why didn't he come out?'

'Lynne said he popped a handful of pills as he left, took whisky with him.'

'She knows?'

'He never came back.'

'But that doesn't mean he's dead.'

John Cutter took the small crown of gold teeth from his chinos and held it out in his palm. Being in his pocket had brought it to a shine. Wet hair fell from her mouth as she looked upon the gold, disbelieving.

'You okay?' he asked. 'You're not going to spew?'

She moved closer, riveted.

'Where did you get it?'

'His fucking head, Deborah, he's dead. It's why you didn't set fire to the house.'

She recoiled at his sharpness and kept twisting her hair. Carefully he put his arm around her.

'Come here.'

He guided her over to the bed. He sat beside her. He hid the teeth in his hand, knocking it against his knee as he thought.

'He always was a greedy fucker.'

'I really didn't know he was in there.'

'How would you? I told Shep his remains are the boy's. Now he knows different. I need to get him on side.'

Deborah frowned at the proposal.

'You think people won't find it hard to believe?'

He patted her on the leg before standing.

'They don't need to believe, they need to accept. I think they'll want to, don't you?'

'Even Lynne?'

'She helped shovel him in. None of us are safe and none of us can talk.' He paused. 'It's a mess, isn't it?'

'He's gone, though. It was worth it.'

He rolled the gold in his palm. 'I'll see Lynne.'

'Why?'

'Explain things, give her this.'

'Will she want it?'

'It's Nugget's nugget.'

'I suppose,' she said.

'He wouldn't want it buried.'

John Cutter dropped it back into his chinos, clinking through handcuffs. Looking back from the door, he gestured awkwardly to the rest of the room. His throat glued up, words sticking.

'You know where everything used to be. Some of it might still be there. The fire's ready to go. Like I said, there's a new bulb. Jenny's room hasn't changed.'

'The cat?'

'Still there.'

Deborah wrinkled her nose.

'It doesn't smell.'

'How?'

'It's desiccated.'

She nodded, sucking on a rat tail, picking at the seam of her jeans. She tried more than once to speak. The words that came out when she managed were scared.

'You want me gone when you get back?'

'Might not be back – depends on Shep.'

'Do you?'

'I ... I've mistreated you. I'd welcome you allowing me the chance to make amends.'

John Cutter opened the door and left, leaving Deborah inside. He hoped she would still be there when he came home, to their home. He got into his car, close to terrified at the mere possibility.

Alexander 'Sandy' Corrigan, 38

*Seven years earlier*

Sandy Corrigan sat in his car with the hot air blowing on the windscreen. He tried the wipers. They were still frozen in place. He almost reached for the scraper and de-icer on the passenger seat but chose instead to open the glove compartment and fight through the contents until he found the remains of a damp packet of cigarettes. Putting one between his lips, he waited for the dashboard lighter to pop out. He applied it to the end of his first in months, sucking hard, needing it to light. Smoke jetted from his nostrils, filling the car. He cracked the windows. It crossed his mind that it might be quicker to walk to the school than it would to wait for the car to defrost. He sucked again and lit another with the glowing tip. He would be late. Only by minutes, minutes he needed, minutes without Dog Evans. The simple act of making this decision eased the tension in his neck and lessened the headache. He took his hat off as the interior warmed.

Just on nine o'clock, Sandy Corrigan stamped his boots clean outside Munson's. Ed Munson picked up a packet of the chewing gum Sandy had favoured since he had quit smoking and placed them on the counter.

'Running late, Sandy.'

'Only a few minutes, they'll live. Twenty please, Ed.'

Sandy's request stopped the flow of Munson's chat. He placed his hand over the gum.

'You're back on them?'

'Afraid so. For the time being, anyway.'

'What happened?' Munson replaced the gum with a packet of smokes.

'A pupil, if you'll believe that.'

'Shep's boy?'

'What have you heard?'

'Mutterings,' said Munson. 'You know how parents can be. Exaggerations, I would imagine.'

'Don't be so sure. Who muttered?'

'Struan was in early on. He was the loudest, but others have said similar.' Munson leant towards Sandy Corrigan, lowering his voice in case another customer entered and overheard. 'I love kids, Sandy, I really do, and not just my grandson. I even feel bad saying this, but I can't warm to Shep's boy.'

'He gives me the fucking heebies. I'm surprised I didn't find my tyres slashed this morning.'

Sandy chose to say no more. But Munson saw it as a way to ask what would otherwise have been an awkward question.

'Did you lock him in the cupboard, really?'

'He usually goes in of his own volition. Yesterday I had to lock the door because he had the rest of the class witless with fear. They wouldn't come in otherwise.'

'The scream? Sounds hellish. Young Struan pished himself?'

Sandy's hand shook as he took a note from his wallet and handed it to Munson.

'Now you know why I'm back on them.'

Munson rang the sale up and handed over change.

'Seems a shame,' he said as he took the freshly peeled cellophane wrap and foil top from Sandy and dropped it into the bin. 'Are you not as well taking a drink as going back on these? It's easier to stop.'

'I might do both and I might not want to stop,' said Sandy, trying for levity.

'Need matches?'

Sandy held up an old lighter as he took a cigarette from the pack. 'Who'd be a teacher, hey?'

'Not me, that's for sure. I'll see you later, Sandy.'

'Aye, probably.'

Sandy Corrigan had filled his lungs with smoke before he left the warmth of the shop. He stopped at the entrance and emptied them.

'You look like a film star, one of they ones from the forties or fifties.'

When he turned back, he saw Ed Munson using his hands to suggest the shape of a cinema screen.

'Snowflakes falling, smoke swirling, artificial light, looking into the night, deep in thought.'

'It's morning.'

'Ach, you know what I mean.'

'Am I the hero or the villain?'

'I'm not sure,' said Ed Munson, as Sandy Corrigan drew again on his cigarette. 'It's a key moment in the film, though.'

Sandy stood wreathed in frame for a second, thinking.

'A crossroads? The moment when the teacher decides if he's cut out for the job or not?'

'Maybe.'

'One bad apple, you'd think I could cope with that, wouldn't you?' Sandy didn't wait for an answer. 'I might just give them the day off. It's drifting hard, they should probably get home while they can.'

'Ach, Sandy man,' said Ed Munson, coming from behind his counter to stand with the teacher and judge the conditions. 'It's nothing. A wee drop of snow. If the papers made it through I'd say the kids will. That's if they don't freeze to death waiting for you to get there.'

'There is that, I suppose.' Sandy crossed the pavement, rock salt crunching beneath his feet, and got back into his car. He waved to Ed Munson as he pulled away.

It was hard going driving against the wind, and the snow appeared to be doing its damnedest to stop him getting to school. Flurries rushed towards him along the full beams, reflecting most of their light back as a bright wall. As slow as he drove he couldn't prevent the back end sliding from his control as he attempted to steer around the corner at the bottom of Main Street. The rear wheel hit the kerbstone, rattling the snow chains that he'd thrown onto the back seat almost a week ago, telling himself he would fit them before the weather really turned. He concentrated as he struggled to maintain the car's forward motion.

Coming straight off the salt marsh, the north-easterly drove the snow horizontally against the schoolhouse. His pupils were huddled in the lee of a sheltering wall, seeking communal warmth. Feeling guilty for keeping them waiting in such hostile conditions, Sandy Corrigan had the door open before his car was stationary, gasping at the biting cold as he got out. Head bowed, he ran to join the class, taking the keys from his pocket as he did so. It was surprisingly peaceful when he reached them, and he saw they weren't gathered against the cold but in a group conversation. What woes today? Looking around, he saw no sign of Dog.

'He ain't here, sir.'

Jonny Raffique faced him, the teeth of his smile visible down the tunnel of his parka hood. Sandy Corrigan couldn't help but smile in response. Other upturned faces showed his relief was infectious. He was cheered by this. The moment was short-lived. A sudden change in the wind direction blasted snow around the corner.

'Aagh, quick,' he said, 'inside before we freeze. I'm sorry I'm late, come on.'

He rushed to the door and had it unlocked in seconds, standing back as he shooed them all inside.

'Quick as you can now, everybody inside, coats off.'

A chorus of coughing and laughing began inside, and complaints about the smell. He assumed it was coming from the storeroom and knew it could be easily remedied. He followed the last child in, looking forward to the day.

'Come on now, calm down.'

He smelled the gas as he raked his hand down the brass switch-plate and realised it was too late to stop or warn the children.

Flying through the air, he saw flames explode through every window. He landed as the roof disappeared, dropping into the classroom under the weight of its snow blanket.

His body being found so far from the school and

the bodies of his charges was enough to indicate guilt. He had killed them and failed to escape, his death an accidental consequence of his actions. This blame was confirmed by the surviving child's account of events: that Sandy Corrigan had arrived late and been desperate to get everybody inside, rushing them into the unlit room of the school. This testimony convinced parents and investigators that he had ensured all the children were inside before he turned on the lights. Disowned by his only surviving relative, Sandy Corrigan was interred in a dank corner behind the church in what had been the old septic tank. His burial was an onerous task carried out by Finnegan. He didn't bother with a service, pissed on the coffin and cursed every shovelful as he filled the hole.

# 25

John Cutter made no attempt to lessen the sound of his approach as he walked back to the murder scene holding the weapon he'd used to kill Dog Evans. He stopped, looking down at Shep, on all fours, almost to the elbows in the boy's grave. He'd been crying. John witnessed the final sobs and sniffs, the attempted wiping of his eyes on his jacket sleeve. He waited. Seconds passed before Shep could lift his head and look him in the eye.

'John?'

'I can't apologise, Shep. I'm sorry for you. Always have been.'

'How has it come to this, John? We used to be friends.'

'Like to think I still was, somehow.'

'You killed my son.'

'It was the right thing to do.'

'After all this time? Why? How?'

'Nothing was right while he was alive. Now, it feels complete.'

'How can killing the last one be the right thing, John? They're all gone now. How can that be complete? It's the opposite of complete.'

Shep's head dropped. John stepped in front of him. Shep's arms were lost in the soil. He was still shaking. John watched his attention move to the scuffed toes of his boots before continuing to the bough, his son's blood, his friend's rigid grip, looking for release.

'Should I close my eyes?' said Shep.

'What?'

'So I don't see it coming.'

Cutter consciously relaxed his hold, steadied his voice. 'It's not.'

Shep gave the briefest of acknowledgements. Shifting his weight, John looked around the glade.

'I don't see Rebecca?'

'She stayed back at the hotel, didn't want to come.'

'I must say that surprises me. I thought she'd want proof more than anybody.'

'Proof?'

'So she could rest easy. I know she's fragile, Shep, and why.'

Shep's silence confirmed Cutter's claim.

'This is what she prayed for,' said Shep. 'Every visit to every church. It isn't right, to pray for this, no matter what.'

'Not for me to say, Shep. You know when my praying days stopped. But if it's what she wanted, it might help; the old Rebecca might come back.'

'I don't know. She's been gone long and far.'

'So have we all.'

'How's Debbie?'

'Debs is in the house: first time in a while. I couldn't say how she is, though; our history's nearly as broken as yours.' In the pause that followed, John Cutter's fists firmed up around the club. 'Tired and lonely would be my best guess. I didn't think about her that much, not at all if I could help it. Was a period she didn't bring out the good in me, I'm afraid.'

'That's sad, John, she always did.'

'Not an easy task.'

'But worth it.'

John Cutter shrugged.

'You happy?' he asked.

'Not often.'

'Leaving didn't help?'

'Running away wasn't the answer.'

'Staying hasn't helped much.'

'When it happens, happiness usually comes from Becky, somehow. Fragile as she is, I believe she's stronger than me.'

'I know that feeling.'

John Cutter sat down next to Shep, their faces inches apart. He could smell the soil, Shep's body, the icy damp in the air and the musty, arrested decay of foliage. He couldn't smell the schoolroom, warm milk, Play-Doh and crayons; or his daughter and wife, soaped and shampooed for parents' evening; or the gas and smoke and stour and sleet of that final day. He remembered the two plastic chairs, one stacked on top of the other so the wee ones could reach the piano keyboard, alone and strangely untouched by the explosion; parents arriving, running, falling, howling, screaming, digging.

'Shep, I think the other night was the answer. Nobody pointed the finger or shied away; it was a collaboration.'

'They wanted to be a part of it?'

'Can you blame them?' Cutter dropped the bough into his lap. He rubbed his face and looked at Shep. 'Hard to hear myself talking this way. I'm supposed to uphold the law. I killed him. We tried to hide him.'

'Do you think it will hold? The collusion?'

'I don't know. It's down to time and conscience; how much people can bear, for how long. I do know that what happened was inevitable, had to happen.'

'Had to?'

'I'm surprised we lasted this long when I think about it. It's been building: every year, every birthday, every day. There are always fresh flowers on one of the graves. Every sighting: being reminded.'

Shep grunted as he pushed harder through the soil, past his elbows, straining with the exertion. He stopped, closed his eyes for a moment before resting his face briefly on the ground. His shoulders moved slightly in response to his fingers' exploration.

'Why are you doing this?'

Shep stopped exploring.

'I need to be telling Becky the truth.'

He withdrew from the grave slowly, pausing before extracting his hands. Crumbs of soil fell from his wrists, cuffs and ridden-up sleeves. He rubbed his fingertips against his thumb, leaving dark sticky smears.

He took his handkerchief and wiped the stickiness away. He sat back on his heels.

'You convinced it was him?'

'No doubt in my mind,' said Cutter, 'or the minds of others. Be no doubt in yours if you read the boy Munson's journal.'

'What I know is enough. Reading it could only be worse,' said Shep.

'I guess. We got a headstone for Sandy Corrigan. That's how sure we are.'

'I tried to love him so much, you know that?'

'I remember it. You doted for two, defended every criticism.'

'I thought he needed me. He wasn't God's little miracle. Becky didn't even believe he was God's.'

'That's how she gave up on him, rather than God?'

'I suppose. Fucked if I'll ever work that one out.'

'She made the right choice in a way.'

John Cutter took out his handcuffs and offered them to Shep. Shep didn't take them.

'Not my job, John.'

'Somebody should. Feels appropriate for it to be you. You're right. What I did won't stay quiet, not forever.'

'You don't think they'll bear the weight of their crime?'

'I don't know. Depends how they view it.'

Shep still made no attempt to take the cuffs. John Cutter put them back.

He held the club out. 'What'll I do with this?'

'Throw it back, let it be; let things be.'

John stood. A strong underarm swing and it was gone.

'I think I'm going to go now, see if Debs is in the house, sit with her if she'll stand me. You be okay?'

Shep put his hand out. John Cutter took it and helped him to his feet.

'Thank you.' Shep rolled his dirty sleeves back down to his wrists. He wiped the grime from his watch; checked it was ticking. 'I'm done here, John. I'll walk out with you.'

As they left the glade, crouching beneath branches

and pushing through the fence, the snow that fell on the grave began to stick. The black iris grew milky. Before long it would be blind.

He thought she was gone and he was downhearted, but it was to be expected. A lot had been broken. He closed the door, disliking the space he shared with no one. Two days ago it had only contained his anger. Now it was wide and open and every corner needed filling, bringing back to life.

'John?'

Her voice surprised him. He was at the foot of the staircase in an instant, looking up at the bulb. The cobwebs were gone.

'Yes?'

'Bring some tools?'

'Okay.'

Snatching a tool roll from the rack, he took the stairs in threes. He stopped at the top.

The cobwebs had been cleared.

The cat was gone.

The landing floor was swept.

The vacuum cleaner was still plugged in.

Jenny's desk had been dusted.

Her window was open. He could smell cool, fresh air upstairs for the first time in years.

Deborah sat on Jenny's bed holding the red boots to her chest.

John stepped into the room as if he was intruding. Deborah patted the bed. Springs creaked and gave way as he sat, tilting them together.

'It looks better,' he said.

'Didn't take much. She was always a tidy girl.'

John placed his tool roll on the bed as he looked around. He lifted Jenny's doll off her pillow. He held it to his nose. Damp, it smelled old and uncared for. He noticed small specks of mould in the fabric and flecks of rust on the zip of the dress.

'She's gone, John.'

'I know.'

He laid the doll back on her pillow. Deborah placed the boots on the foot of the bed and turned to him.

'I want to come back.'

John nodded.

'You want me back?'

'I do.'

He took her hand and held it. She spoke with hope.

'We can fix our room.'

'I'll fix it. I'll make it new.'

'I'll help you.'

'Rather you didn't see it,' he said.

'I need to, or I won't be able to help.'

'It's not pretty.'

'Neither am I any more.'

'I disagree.'

He pulled her closer. She fitted into her space, rested her head against him. Running his hand over her cheek, he put his nose to her head, welcoming familiar smells back. She spoke quietly, without raising her head.

'John?'

'Yes.'

'Do you think we'll be okay? I mean, everything?'

'We can only try.'

'But what about Shep?'

'I think it's as over for Shep as it is for us. I'd be surprised to see Shep or Rebecca again.'

Deborah looked at him.

'But we can leave him there? Forget about him?'

'Like I said, we can try.'

As John shifted, the nugget fell from his trousers onto the bed. He picked it up.

'At least Nug can have a proper burial,' Deborah said. 'We don't have to pretend his remains are the dog's.'

He stared at the gold but his thoughts were elsewhere.

'What is it, John?'

'The priest.'

'I don't think he'll say anything.'

'Makes you say that?'

'He's got as much to confess as us.'

John waited.

'We talked,' she said.

He let it go, knowing there was more.

Shep was glad of the empty room. He saw Rebecca's note and the luggage, packed and ready. He read the note and scrunched it into the bin. He stripped, pushing his soiled clothes into one of the hotel's plastic laundry bags, and stepped into the scalding shower in the steam-filled bathroom. Using his toothbrush he cleaned beneath his nails, then scrubbed every inch of skin that had been in contact with the grave until his arms were pink and sore and he could no longer tolerate the heat of the water.

Opening his bag and swapping clean for dirty, Shep

dressed. Once ready, he lifted their luggage from the bed and took it downstairs.

In the foyer, he hit the desk bell with just enough force to make it heard. Glen was still chewing when he came through the door.

'I'm sorry,' said Shep. 'I didn't know you were eating.'

Glen waved his concerns away as he swallowed the chewed mouthful.

'Excuse me. Not at all, we're practically finished. Your wife is over at the church, if you're looking for her.'

'I know. That's where I usually find her.'

'She made me feel so bad for not having bibles in the rooms. A situation I'm going to rectify asap.'

'I wouldn't rush to fill your rooms with bibles; not many need them. Not as much as they need good food, a comfortable bed and a hot shower. All of which I've enjoyed.'

'Thank you,' said Glen. 'That means a lot.'

'I mean it,' said Shep, as he took out his wallet. 'I'd like to settle our bill.'

'You'll be leaving tonight?'

'Thought we'd try and beat the snow, before it gets too heavy. Don't want to get stuck here.'

'I understand. Like they say, could be a day, could be a lifetime.'

'They said it right.'

'Sally mentioned … You get everything you needed done?'

'Pretty much,' said Shep. 'Thank you. I'll recommend you to anybody I know coming out this way. You're just what this place needs, you and Sally.'

'Thank you again. I'll pass that on to her.'

Glen looked genuinely pleased as he processed Shep's payment.

Outside, Shep tossed the bags onto the back seat of the car. Closing the door, he pulled a half-cigar from his pocket. Looking across the road, he changed his mind, put it back and headed for the church.

The moment he stepped inside, he saw Wittin making his way from the vestry. The priest had cleaned the blood from his face and was wearing his collar. He eyed Shep briefly before stepping into the confessional.

Shep lowered the door latch quietly. Apart from the burning candles, there was no sign of Rebecca. He knew she was waiting to confess. He hesitated, remembering how closed she had been when he'd asked what she prayed for. Bending to loosen his laces, he stepped out of his shoes and carried them to the pew closest to the confessional, leaving damp sock-prints on the floor. Wittin's voice was the first he heard.

'Are you sure you want to do this? It can wait until …'

'Until?'

'Things have settled down and you know how you feel. Sure, it's been a difficult time.'

'I know how I feel.'

Rebecca's voice was clear and strong and sure. Shep hadn't heard such certainty for a long time. He had grown accustomed to the sound of her fear.

'Okay then,' said Wittin.

'Bless me, Father, for I have sinned. It has been five years since my last confession.'

There was a pause where Wittin's response should have been.

'You're not going to ask me,' she said.

'All right. Why so long since your last confession?'

'Because I saw no point confessing to a sin I would commit over and over again.'

'There was no contrition?'

'None.'

'You sure now? You really weren't able to reject the sin and resolve never to commit it again?'

'No, Father.'

'What was this sin?'

'I prayed every day for the death of my son, Douglas Evans.'

'And now he's dead. So that's it?'

Rebecca didn't answer straight away. Shep slipped his feet back into his shoes. He could hear the priest losing patience with her and wanted to be ready when she came out.

'Yes,' she said, as if it all should be obvious to him. 'I no longer need to pray and I can confess.'

'You really think it's that simple?'

'Why wouldn't it be?'

'Because it isn't just a case of you confessing, of saying the words. Your love of God can only be reborn with true repentance. You do understand?'

'I do repent. I am truly sorry.'

'Okay then; do you regret his death?'

'No.'

'Asking God for his death?'

'I had no one else.'

260

'Even though each request was a mortal sin, an offence to him and the grace of the soul?'

Rebecca was silent.

'Do you really think God answered your prayers and caused the death of another human being?'

Again, Rebecca failed to answer Wittin's question. Her demurring appeared to calm him down slightly and to Shep's ears his tone became priestly, conciliatory.

'He could never answer a prayer like that, could he?'

'No.'

'I'm glad we agree. Are you still clear about what you're confessing?'

'I'm less sure.'

'Of the exact nature of the sin?'

'Yes.'

'Would you be needing more time, to examine your conscience?'

'Wishing him dead was a sin, I know that. But asking God's help to that end was a far greater sin, wasn't it?'

Shep and Wittin had both heard Rebecca's doubt.

'I would say so, if one mortal sin could carry more weight than another. I know it's been a long time, and this is hard, but you'll feel better when you receive the Lord's mercy and you are forgiven. We'll go slowly so.'

'I'm sorry, Father.'

'That's all right, it's why I'm here.'

'No, I'm sorry. I can't ask for God's forgiveness.'

'Come on now. Why ever not? We're almost there.'

'Because I'm not sorry. I'm glad he's dead and I know it's wrong.'

Wittin didn't respond. Shep could hear him fidgeting, at a loss.

'You don't need to say anything,' said Rebecca. 'Thank you for listening.'

'I am sorry for you, child. I want to help you. But what you asked him for, that's a burden you'll have to carry alone.'

'Nothing to the one I carried.'

'I hope you have the strength.'

'I'm feeling stronger.'

Wittin sighed. They both knew it was over.

Rebecca stepped out of the confessional to find Shep sitting in the nearest pew, waiting for her.

'You were listening?'

'I heard,' he said, stepping into the aisle.

'He knew you were here?' Rebecca indicated Wittin's side of the confessional. He didn't come out.

'Let's go home, Becky.'

Rebecca went to Shep and hugged him harder than she had for years. He gathered her in.

'Can you call me Becky?'

'Like I used to?'

'Yes.'

'From now on?'

'Yes.'

'Okay then.'

He kissed her.

'I love you, Shep.'

'I know.' She blinked as he pushed her hair from her face, tucking it behind her ear. 'You're looking well.'

'I'm looking tired and old.'

'Not from here.'

She kissed him. They moved as one to the door and left the church without looking back.

Shep handed Becky the half-opened woollen blanket. She was already swaddling herself as he closed the car door. The windows were slowly demisting. He took the chance to spend five minutes with his cigar, the snow and the quiet of the village. When the windows had cleared and the snow on the bonnet had begun to melt as it landed, he flipped his wet cigar stub into the gutter and slipped his jacket off. He laid it across the bags on the back seat. He was about to get into the warmth of the car when he saw movement through the hotel window. Glen and Sally were both waving. He waved back, not blaming them for staying inside. Looking at them, he hoped they had what it would take to drag this village out of the past. He imagined himself in the future, a regular customer on Sunday mornings, having coffee and a pastry while he read the papers, enjoying a cigar on the hotel steps, talking to Sally again.

Moments later, he eased the car away from the hotel kerb and drove up the hill. Becky was asleep before the lights from Struan House left the rear view. She didn't wake until he guided the car between snow poles, laying fresh tracks across the car park of the inn.

'Want me to leave it running?' he said as he applied the handbrake.

'Please.'

'I won't be long, a minute or so.'

'Okay.' Her eyes were already closing again.

Inside, the bar was empty. The only sound was the crackle of the freshly stoked fire in the hearth. When Bill stood and turned around, a tin bucket of hot ashes in his hand, he was surprised to see Shep.

'Shep?'

'That's a good fire you've got going, Bill.'

'Never know on a night like this. Somebody might make it here and need it. I've got soup, tea, whisky and an open fire. That would warm anybody up.' He frowned. 'Thought you'd be a while longer, I have to say.'

He put the bucket down on the hearthstone as Shep sought a handshake.

'I just came to say goodbye, Bill. I don't know if I'll ever be up this way again.'

'Where's the good lady?'

'Waiting in the car. Pretending to sleep.'

'Nonsense; let me …'

As Bill made to go by Shep, his intention to repair the last meeting as best he could, Shep put his hand out, stopping him.

'She's fragile. It'll take time.'

Bill stopped, met Shep's gaze; acquiesced.

'Okay.'

'Thank you.'

'How did the funeral go?'

'Not easy.'

'My sincere condolences, Shep, to the both of you.'

'Thanks, Bill.'

'Was there a good turnout?'

'Most of the village saw him buried.'

'Well, that's something, isn't it?'

'Yeah, that was something.'

'At least he was liked. You can take consolation from that.'

Shep shook Bill's hand. 'Thanks again, Bill.'

He didn't look back as he left the inn.

He got into the car, kissed his sleeping wife, put the wipers back on and headed south.

# Acknowledgements

Dog Evans was born in the bar of the Plockton Inn. Michael Campbell and Stephen Burt helped with the birth. John Weir gave me the use of his Millport flat to get to first. Val Penny was up for being first reader. All at Freight, particularly, Adrian Searle, Rodge Glass, Robbie Guillory and Persephone Lock. Ben Willis and all at Orion. Nicola Barr, for taking a chance on the writer of this dark novel.

Merci – Cleremont Ferrand, Admiral Flotant for the invitation. Francois Andrieux, Camille, Baptiste and the cats, were generous with hospitality, guidance, good cheese and the best bread. Sophie, Maela, Annabelle and Florence, drove me, supported me and were good company. Francois Nugier and Michael Bourrier almost made me want to teach. Jean Christophe and Beatrice welcomed me into their home for truffade, wine and brandy.

*'You know what I've learned, you know what I've learned?*
*Some people do love you when you are down and out,*
*and they are the people I will value for my ever.'*

Jonny Murray, Bovy and Caroline MacKinnon, Jeremy Donald, Mum, Anne and Jim, Beth and Brian, Carole, Ava and Honor.